Wed

to a

SEAL

HOT SEALS

Cat Johnson

ISBN-13: 978-1523378753
ISBN-10: 1523378751

CHAPTER ONE

Which one?

That was the only unknown weighing on Rocky Mangiano's mind as he swallowed a gulp of beer and perused the choices before him.

After being home for something like a grand total of seven days over the past seven months, which girl to choose to spend a little time with tonight wasn't a bad dilemma to have.

Rocky was there alone, but that didn't mean he'd be lonely, thanks to the plethora of ladies employed by the strip club.

His teammates weren't around, not even the few single ones who he might have persuaded to join him. Since they were finally home from back-to-back assignments—hopefully here to stay for at least a little while—the guys had scattered to see family.

Brody Cassidy was visiting his folks in Alabama, but there were hints that a girl there who was more of a draw than good old Mom and Dad.

James "Mack" MacIntyre had been summoned by his father to . . . somewhere. Rocky wasn't sure where Mack's dad lived, not that it mattered. His teammate was busy for the weekend.

His usual drinking buddies' absence wouldn't put a damper on Rocky's evening. He hadn't come to the club seeking male companionship.

No, sir, he certainly had not. He was here for company of the female variety.

He feasted on the colorful scene before him.

Red. Blue. Purple. Gold. The strippers' sequined costumes, designed to catch the eyes of the male patrons, reflected the stage lights, sending thousands of shards of reflected light through the air to where they landed and danced on every surface.

Warring with the sequins for attention was the glitter. It coated every inch of the girls' exposed skin, skin which came in every shade from ivory to bronze to deep cocoa brown.

Sure, it was frigging annoying to go home from the club covered in glitter and cheap perfume. Both seemed nearly impossible to get off his skin and his clothes. But it would be far more annoying to finally get home safely from a mission only to sit in his room all alone.

They'd been through some rough shit this last round. He needed to blow off a little steam. All he needed to figure out was who to do it with.

Focused on the creative gyrations of the girl currently on stage, he took another sip of the beer, happy and content to take his time in this decision.

Was enjoying drinking alone a sign that he had a problem? Nah. He didn't think so in this instance.

Besides, he was far from alone. Hell, he was surrounded by people—both men and women—and for a change not even one of them was shooting at him.

That in itself was worthy of celebrating with a drink … or two.

Two. That was an idea. Maybe he wouldn't choose just one girl. He'd been overseas so much this year with no expenses except the small storage unit where his shit lived when he was away that he'd been stockpiling his pay.

He could more than afford a couple of visits to the back for private lap dances tonight.

"Hey there, big guy." The sultry words, spoken low and close to his ear from behind him, cut through the music being pumped out of the sound system and directly to his gut.

Rocky turned in his seat to get a look at the familiar bleached blonde. He recognized her as one of Brody's past favorites.

Of course, that was before Brody's very recent aversion to the strip club, which Rocky suspected was due to the addition of that girl back home in Alabama. Not that his buddy had willingly come right out and admitted that. It was like pulling teeth getting anything personal out of Brody.

Some guys kept things close to the vest. Brody was one of them, but the signs were there. The man who never took leave had done so an awfully lot lately. That, to Rocky, had serious relationship written all over it.

Rocky, on the other hand, couldn't be bothered keeping secrets in his personal life. He had to keep too many secrets from family and friends for work already.

With women he liked to be open about things when he could be, such as feelings and plans for the future . . . or lack thereof.

That's what he planned to do with this lovely young lady who'd come to seek out his company.

Smiling, he turned more fully to face her. "Hey there, sweetheart."

"Alone tonight? Where are your usual buddies?" She ran one long, colorfully polished fingernail down his arm.

"Sadly, quite a few of them have fallen." When her eyes widened in horror, Rocky knew he'd better clarify his statement. "To the love bug, I mean. They're fine. Don't worry. Just otherwise engaged."

This place was located right outside one of the gates of the base. These girls were very much aware that sailors made up probably ninety percent of their clientele. He should have realized she'd jump to the wrong conclusion.

She pressed one hand to the glittery bare skin above her exposed cleavage and blew out a breath. "You scared me. I'm glad to hear they're okay. And I'm very glad you're here."

Her smile looked almost genuine. Hell, maybe it was. After all, if she played her cards right she'd be walking away with a nice tip from him tonight.

That was something to smile about.

Her eyes dropped down his body, skimming over the muscles of his chest beneath the T-shirt he knew was a size too small. Not his fault. It was made of cheap cotton and shrank in the laundry.

Now he was happy it had, if the admiration in her eyes was any indication of how he looked while wearing it. All of those hours of PT were good for more than just chasing down bad guys.

She leaned lower, giving him a nice view as she draped her arms over each of his shoulders. A cloud of perfume engulfed him and he tried not to breathe too deeply for fear he'd choke.

"Wanna go in back?" she asked.

"Sure. Can I finish my beer first?" Rocky hated warm beer.

He'd drink it warm—he had many times abroad—but while home in the good old US of A he was going to enjoy the amenities to the fullest. Ice-cold beer was one of them.

Besides, he was in no rush to hurry the night along. What did he have to do?

Not much besides head back to his bare barracks room. Maybe watch a little television. Have another beer. Go to sleep all alone.

Not a hell of a lot of inspiration to get moving.

She lifted one thin brow as if surprised he hadn't jumped up and followed her back immediately. "Oh, okay."

The stripper glanced around, as if deciding if she should waste her time waiting for him, or move on to more promising hunting grounds.

Fine with him either way. There were plenty of girls to go around, just like there were plenty of patrons—the place was particularly packed tonight for some reason. If Rocky knew what the date was he could maybe figure out why.

It was probably some sort of a holiday weekend

but he couldn't be sure. The months had started to blur together. Over the past half a year he'd been on the terrorist tour of the world—Turkey, Nigeria, Iraq, Syria.

Uncle Sam called and Rocky went, wherever and whenever he was told.

Tonight, for once, no one was telling him what to do and he was going to take full advantage of the freedom. If wanting to finish his beer lost him Blondie's attention, so be it. There were more fish in the sea. Colorful, glittery ones of all shapes and sizes.

Her eyes flicked to a man at a nearby table before she said to Rocky, "Flag me down when you're ready."

"Sure. No problem." Rocky lifted his beer to her in a toast and watched her go, not all that heartbroken.

Again he glanced around him and took note of the sheer number of men filling the place.

For lack of anything else to be concerned about, curiosity got the best of him. There was one simple way to find out the date. He stood for long enough to get his cell out of the pocket of his jeans.

Sitting again, he hit the button that should have resulted in the phone lighting up and telling him both the date and the time. Nothing happened. It remained dark.

Frowning, he pushed the button again. The cell lit just long enough to show him the dead battery alert.

He sighed, wishing he could just leave the phone dead and enjoy the evening.

He was home. Drinking. Well fed. Single and carefree. Barracks room though it was, he was going to sleep in his own bed, after showering in his own bathroom. His bills were paid and his career was kick-ass.

His life—at least for tonight—was just about perfect except for the fact that as long as he was an active duty SEAL, a text from command could come at any time.

Rocky tracked the progress of one of his favorite girls as she crossed the stage. Jasmine.

He could finish his beer and then grab her for a private dance. *Then* the evening would be perfect. He smiled at the thought.

Life was good.

Lifting his beer, he downed the last of it and stood. He'd go outside and plug his phone into the charger in the dashboard. He could check for any messages from command. Then he could come back inside and leave the phone charging while he enjoyed some attention from sweet Jasmine for a little while.

Command could wait the twenty minutes or so it would take for him to check the cell again. He was right outside the gate. He could be back on base and in the meeting room in five minutes from here.

Happy with that plan, Rocky stood and headed for the door.

CHAPTER TWO

Isabel Alvarez. Single mother. Illegal immigrant. Stripper.

Her bio wasn't exactly stellar and not at all what she'd planned when she'd left Cuba as a starry eyed girl heading off to university in America.

How had this become her life?

Isabel stared into the mirror in the dressing room of the club, but the dark-haired woman with big brown frightened-looking eyes and tawny skin reflected back didn't supply any answers.

"You leaving for the night already?" Jasmine reached for a towel and cut her gaze to Isabel.

"I have to. The babysitter can't stay any later."

Jasmine nodded. "I hear you. Thank God babysitters make far less an hour than I can earn here or I'd never make ends meet."

As Isabel hung her costume in her locker, she watched Jasmine swipe on a layer of red lipstick.

Even though the woman had worked as long a day shift as Isabel had, she apparently was staying for at least part of the night shift too. "You're going back out on the floor?"

"Oh yeah."

"You working a double?" As mentally and physically exhausting as this job could get, Isabel should be working double shifts herself. She needed the money, but she needed her babysitter to be able to work when she did and that wasn't happening today.

"Nah, I'm not staying all night but I saw one of my best customers out there. It'll be worth it to stay late for this guy. After being gone for a while, those Navy guys are more than willing to part with their money. SEALs especially. They work hard but let me tell you they play even harder. This one's not too hard on the eyes either. Definitely won't be a hardship showing him a little extra attention in the back room." Jasmine's red lips tipped up in a smile.

Isabel lifted a brow as she listened to Jasmine's plan for the evening. "Didn't you tell me the day I started that if a customer told me he was a SEAL, then he was a liar?"

Since that had been only a couple of months ago, she was sure she remembered the lecture correctly.

Jasmine nodded. "I did and it's true."

Confused, Isabel shook her head. "Then why—"

"He never told me what he does. Never told me anything but a nickname and believe me I asked. That right there would have told me he is what I think he is. But besides that, he's got the SEAL insignia tattooed right there." Jasmine rubbed her fingers high on the front of her thigh to indicate where this guy's tattoo was.

"Oh." Wide-eyed, Isabel didn't question how her coworker had seen this man's upper thigh or when. Some things were better unasked.

Though Jasmine's cash earnings being so high made a lot more sense now.

"All right. I better get back out there before somebody else gets to him first. Have a good night, sweetie. I know I will." Jasmine winked and turned on one high heel toward the door.

"'Night." Isabel watched her coworker leave, as her own emotions roiled within her.

She couldn't do this job. Not if working here meant that men expected her to do more than just dance. What Jasmine was obviously not only willing, but eager to do.

Of course, Isabel was no virgin or a saint. The fact she'd had a baby without the benefit of having a husband proved that. But to give a stranger anything more than the standard lap dance was beyond her.

At least right now it was. If things got any worse in her life who knew what desperate measures she'd resort to. Apparently she didn't make the best decisions.

Her ex, Tito, and everything that had happened in Miami proved that. And even though Isabel loved her daughter beyond reason and would do anything for her, little Lola's mere existence was proof of her bad decision making as well.

The whole course of events that led to Isabel being here—in Virginia, in this strip club—proved she needed to keep her head on straight and make better choices.

From now on, she would.

Resolute, she reached for the make-up remover. She had to get back to her apartment, but she wasn't about to walk in looking like a stripper . . . even if that was exactly what she was.

The babysitter—her neighbor's thirteen year old daughter Hannah—didn't know the details about what Isabel did for work and she intended to keep it that way.

It took some time to get all the make-up, not to mention the glitter off. She made do with just making sure her face was not glistening with the telltale stripper adornment.

Her clothes would cover the rest of her skin so Isabel could wait until she got home to shower.

When she was finally presentable, she grabbed her bag and headed out the back door tonight. It meant a longer walk to where she'd parked her car, but she figured it was easier to leave through the back than to work her way across the club packed with customers to go out the front door the way she usually did.

It wasn't very late at night, but sunset came early this time of year.

She stepped into the darkness and glanced around her. Habit, she supposed. Being on the run tended to make a person extra vigilant.

Though if she were really being careful she shouldn't be back behind the club where it was pitch black and there was no one who would see her if she needed help.

Feeling uncomfortable being so alone in the dark, she made a decision. Next shift she'd deal with the crowd and exit through the front where there were plenty of people around. Safety in numbers.

She hustled a little faster through the darkness but breathed easier when she rounded the corner and was greeted by the warm glow of the parking lot lights overhead.

There were a couple of people hovering around the front entrance smoking cigarettes. The engine of a parked car rumbled to life as the headlights flipped on, while a pick-up truck pulled into the entrance and slowed to a stop, obviously waiting to take the car's space in the crowded lot.

Blowing out a breath, she tried to calm her racing heart, the result of her frightened sprint from the back door to her car.

She'd gotten herself scared for nothing. Even so, she was definitely leaving by the front door from now on. No reason to take any chances.

As she dug in her bag for her key, which she realized should have been out and in her hand before she ever left the building, the owner of the truck was opening the front door of the club. As he held it, the two smokers ground out their cigarettes and followed him in.

She was alone again, but at least it wasn't dark.

Grateful when she felt the key ring in her purse, she pulled it out.

All this stress couldn't be good for her health. People had heart attacks even at only twenty-one, didn't they?

Even if she didn't fall over from cardiac arrest, her letting herself worry obsessively could probably dry up her milk. Not only would she have to deal with an unhappy three-month old, she'd also have to spend money on formula. Not to mention losing her best asset at the club—her double D-cups brought on by breastfeeding. Any reduction in her tips would be financially devastating.

She was being silly. Again. There'd be no heart attack. No drying up of milk. No getting attacked in the dark not far outside the gates of a US Naval base.

If anything defeated her, it would be her own mind and self-doubt. Isabel realized that. Now she just had to figure out what to do about it.

Sighing, she opened the car door and tossed her bag inside before sliding behind the steering wheel. Soon she'd be home. She'd kiss her baby, have a hot shower and a warm meal and feel a hundred percent better.

Turning the key in the ignition, she waited for the car to start but nothing happened.

Nothing at all.

No sputtering. No whining. No sounds of an engine trying to come to life.

Panic gripped her anew. What could be wrong?

How should she know? Cars were not her area of expertise. She'd been in school for biology. Pre-med to be exact. If she ever got the mess her life had become cleaned up, she wanted to be a doctor.

Even one year short of earning her undergraduate degree, healing a human body seemed far easier than fixing a combustion engine.

She could reason this out. She was a smart woman. She took the key out and checked the gear shift. It was in Park so that wasn't it.

Pressing the brake pedal, she slid the key back in and turned.

Again, she wasn't rewarded with the sound she desperately wanted to hear.

A knock on the window right next to her head had her jumping in the seat. She peered out and saw nothing but the broad torso of a man blocking her view of all else out the side window, until he bent low and made a motion for her to roll down the glass.

Afraid to open the window to the bearded stranger, she yelled, "The car won't start."

He nodded. "I know. If you let me take a look at the engine, maybe I can figure out why. Pop the hood."

The whole situation had the feeling of enormity. As if the decision she made next could mean her own life or death.

The front door of the club swung wide and a single man stepped out. She saw the flash of a lighter as he leaned against the building and took a drag from the cigarette.

She was being foolish. This man obviously wasn't trying to kill or kidnap her from the front of a busy club. He'd wanted her to roll down the window so they could talk about her car without yelling and he needed her to unlatch the hood so he could look for a problem.

All reasonable requests, and she'd met them with suspicion. But she was a woman alone and he was a man—a large man by the looks of him—so he'd just have to get over her suspicion.

She reached down and struggled to find the release for the hood beneath the dash. She finally had to give in and admit she couldn't find it in the dark. All the while, he stood by, arms crossed, waiting.

He didn't move except to step back when she unlocked the door so she could open it. Once she did, the dome light flashed on.

She didn't have time to look for the latch before he'd already taken a step forward. He swung the door wider, reached down and pulled on the lever. The hood released with a loud *pop*.

"Don't try to start it until I say. Okay?" He waited for her answer, probably starting to doubt her mental capacity since she was acting like an idiot.

"Okay."

Once he seemed convinced he could trust her to follow instructions, he stepped around to the front of the car and she lost sight of him as he raised the hood.

Now that the fear of bodily harm was passing, the more real concern of what she'd do if her car was broken took over. She didn't have any money saved for emergencies. Certainly not enough for a big repair bill from a service station.

"Okay, give it a go."

Wanting to do the right thing, she decided it was best to confirm first. "You mean try to start it?"

He walked into view. "Yeah. Turn the key, but don't pump the gas. You'll flood it."

She did as he'd asked and the car rumbled to life. Her eyes drifted closed as she said a silent prayer of thanks and let herself breathe again.

He slammed the hood and walked back to her. "It was a loose wire. It should be good now."

"Thank you so much. I mean it. You really saved me." She couldn't help but eye the size of the man's forearm as he leaned on the top of her open door.

He smiled from beneath a thick beard that made him look even more manly than his muscles did. "My pleasure. Always happy to help a lady in need."

Isabel hadn't felt like a lady in a long time, but she nodded anyway. "Well, thank you. I appreciate it."

"You're welcome." His gaze held hers before he extended his arm. "I'm Rocky, by the way."

She hesitated before shaking his hand, reluctant to give him her real name but feeling too guilty to lie since he had fixed her car.

Finally, she fought back the irrational fear and said, "Isabel."

"Isabel. Pretty name. You work here?"

His question gave her pause. It was ridiculous since she was in the parking lot of the strip club and it was pretty obvious she did work here, but for some reason she hadn't wanted him to know that. "Yes. But I'm done for today."

"Maybe I'll see you around sometime. Have a good night." He tipped his dark head.

"Goodnight."

Taking a step back, he slammed her door and turned away.

She watched as he walked to a truck, reached into his pocket and pulled out keys and a cell phone. He opened the door and leaned inside the cab to fiddle with something. He emerged shortly, slammed the door and clicked the locks closed.

Heading back toward the entrance to the building, he glanced up at her car. She felt his eyes on her through the windshield.

Not only had she been caught watching this guy when she had no reason to, but now he was probably wondering if she had some other problem with the car.

Isabel hurried to shift into Reverse and backed out of the space.

Glancing up as she shifted into Drive, she saw he'd gone back inside.

Maybe there were genuinely nice guys to be found, even at a strip club. Or maybe her instincts were still as bad as they'd been when she'd trusted Tito.

It didn't really matter either way. She had to go. As it was she was going to be late getting home to relieve Hannah.

Keeping herself and her daughter safe was Isabel's only concern at the moment. Handsome strangers were not in her plans for the future.

CHAPTER THREE

Isabel woke and stretched, feeling lazy. She had the day off. At least off from working at the club. She still had a mountain of laundry to do, groceries to buy, and a week's worth of meals to prepare.

She'd already learned that eating take-out drained her bank account faster than cooking herself. But if she planned wisely, she could cook enough on her day off to freeze meals to eat for the rest of the week.

A soft cry from the crib in the corner caught her attention. Lola was awake. That had probably been what knocked Isabel out of her peaceful and much needed slumber to begin with.

She added change, feed and bathe her daughter to the list of chores for the day and resigned herself that it was time to get out of bed.

Swinging her legs over the edge of the mattress, she stood and felt the tingling in her feet. A long shift in stripper heels took more than one night's sleep to recover from.

That was why she earned the big bucks, she supposed. If it were easy, everyone would do it.

Yeah, right. Spinning on a pole in a G-string while men ogled was a real dream job.

With a sarcastic snort, she moved to the crib and smiled at her daughter.

"Good morning, *nena*." Isabel had vowed to herself that her daughter would grow to speak and understand both Spanish and English equally well, just as her *abuela* had done with her in Cuba.

Thoughts of home and memories of her late grandmother had Isabel feeling nostalgic. Maybe she'd cook her *abuela's frijoles negros* today.

Making the Cuban black beans was time consuming—she'd have to let the beans soak all day—but luckily she had all day and the effort would be well worth it.

One day Isabel would teach her daughter to make the dish . . . when her life was normal again. As she lifted Lola from the crib she had to believe that day would come.

When Lola was clean and dressed but Isabel was still in her own pajamas, a knock on the apartment door sent her running to see who it was.

A quick glance through the peephole revealed her babysitter Hannah. Isabel unlocked and opened the door.

"Hey. I didn't forget to pay you last night, did I?" She had been pretty tired, not to mention shaken from the car trouble. It wouldn't surprise her if she had forgotten to pay the babysitter.

"Nope, you paid me but I forgot something. When I remembered this morning, my mom said I had to come right over and tell you."

"Oh, okay. Come on in." Isabel backed up and let the girl into the apartment. "What did you forget?"

"Some guy stopped by looking for you."

"What guy?" She'd paid the rent already this month so it shouldn't be the landlord. A feeling of dread filled Isabel. "What did he look like? Can you describe him?"

Hannah's brow wrinkled. "Um, dark hair. He had an accent, kind of like yours actually. His name was something like Rocco maybe?"

With every addition to Hannah's description, Isabel's heart beat faster. She swallowed hard and said, "Tito?"

Hannah's eyes widened with triumph. "Yeah, that was it. He said to tell you he stopped by and that he'd be back."

"Did he say when he'd be back?" It was amazing she could even ask the question as her stomach rolled.

She'd rather throw up than draw more details out of this girl who'd unwittingly dropped the worst news Isabel could have possibly received.

"I think he just said soon."

Isabel glanced toward the bedroom where Lola was playing in her crib with some toys. "Hannah, I need you to think and try and remember. Where exactly was Lola when he was here?"

"In the bedroom."

"You're sure?"

"Yes." Hannah nodded. "I remember because it was after she had her dinner bottle so she was already sleeping and I was watching TV."

Trying not to hyperventilate, Isabel glanced around the living room. Had Lola's baby bottle been out in the living room where Tito could have seen it? Would he have noticed if it had been?

"Did he come in?" She tried to keep the panic out of her voice.

"No. I left the chain on the door like my mother taught me to do when a stranger knocks."

"That's smart. Thank you." As she feigned calm her mind spun. She had to get out of there and fast before he came back.

More, she had to hide Lola and all evidence of her existence. Isabel had worked too hard to keep the baby a secret from her ex. She'd sacrificed too much to have it all be for nothing now.

"Thank you for telling me, Hannah. I've, uh, got some things I need to do. Tell your mother thank you too, for sending you over."

"Sure. You need me to sit again later when you do your errands or whatever?"

"Um, no. I'm good. I'll bring Lola with me." There were a thousand things to do and Isabel had no idea how much time she had to do them before Tito came back. She needed to move and now.

Opening the door while holding her breath, Isabel glanced into the hallway, only breathing again when she saw it was empty.

"See you later, Hannah."

"Sure. See ya." The young girl went on her way with no clue she'd been in contact with the one man who could make Isabel's whole world a living nightmare. He already had, but it could get a lot worse.

After locking and chaining the door, she ran to the bedroom and grabbed the diaper bag. It was big, but not nearly large enough for everything Lola would need for the long term. Even so, Isabel shoved a box of wipes and as many clean diapers as would fit.

In the outside pocket, she wedged in the few clean shirts still in the drawer.

Feeling bad for wrenching Lola from everything familiar to her, she squeezed in her daughter's favorite stuffed animal.

Glancing down, she realized she couldn't drive in what she was wearing. She swapped her pajama pants for jeans and left on the shirt she'd worn to sleep.

She should put on a bra before she left but there wasn't time. Every moment felt like a bomb ticking down toward detonation. She tossed a bra in her purse to put on later and then ran to grab both the diaper bag and the baby.

What was she going to do?

Get out of the apartment was number one. Tito had discovered where she lived, somehow.

Virginia should have been far enough from Miami. It obviously wasn't.

He would always find her. She knew that with certainty.

It was risky since he wasn't a man who let what he considered his property go easily, but she would have to face him. Tell him to leave her alone, but she had to do that alone. If he knew of Lola's existence Isabel would never be free.

That meant she had to hide Lola someplace safe until she could deal with Tito. How she'd do that she had no idea but she'd have to figure it out.

She'd also have to make sure he was back in Miami and done with stalking her before it would be safe to bring Lola back here, or to whatever new place she moved to in hopes he wouldn't find that one.

Dammit, she'd liked this place too. The neighbors were kind and the babysitting was a huge plus. It allowed her to work.

There was no time to think of all that now. She had to find a place to hide Lola.

Some of the girls at the club had kids. Jasmine for one. She'd have to beg to get one of them to take Lola for a little while. Isabel was the new girl at the club, but she had no other options.

With that flimsy plan in mind, she reached for the doorknob and remembered what she'd forgotten.

Food.

The breast pump was already in her tote bag since she carried it with her so she could pump at work during a long shift. But she should grab the bottles she'd already pumped and stored in the fridge for Hannah to give Lola while she was working.

But the breast milk needed to be kept chilled and she didn't have a cooler.

With the feeling of time being against her, Isabel ran to the kitchen.

Weighed down by the baby on one hip and the diaper bag and her purse hooked tenuously on the opposite shoulder, she reached into a cabinet and grabbed for the balled up plastic grocery bags stowed there.

Ice cubes tossed inside the bag with the bottles would have to be good enough for now. She double bagged her makeshift cooler and then tied off the top.

With her hands full, she somehow managed to get the door open.

Again her heart raced as she peeked into the hallway. If she had less of a burden to carry, she'd consider going out the window and using the fire escape just to avoid running into Tito. In fact, as panic gripped her she did consider it.

No. Too risky. She was carrying too much to climb safely and making two trips would only slow her down.

She pulled the door closed behind her. The car keys were in her purse. If she could get out of her building and to where she'd parked last night without him showing up, they'd be free.

Then she could drive directly to the club. It would be open by now. Who was working? She couldn't remember. She'd have to park around the back to hide the car and sneak in with the baby in case Tito had discovered where she'd worked as well as where she lived.

She danced under the name Roxy, not her real name, so maybe her place of work was still a secret. Chances were good if he knew about her job at the club he'd have shown up there when he didn't find her home and as far as she knew he hadn't been there.

If he had been, Isabel had no doubt he would have dragged her off the stage mid-dance and she'd have the resulting bruises today.

He definitely would have knocked her around for running out on him and for stripping. He was a man who used his fists to solve his problems.

That thought had her feeling sick to her stomach.

Mingled plans and fears swirled through her mind as she ran down the hall as quickly as she could without dropping anything or making Lola cry.

The staircase frightened her the most. Being caught halfway down within its narrow walls would be like a trap.

If he was coming up while she was going down there'd be nowhere to hide. No escaping him.

Tito would be able to move far more quickly than she could while carrying a baby.

She made it down the stairs but she was desperate and near hyperventilating when she reached the bottom. There she slowed, pushing the door to the street open just a bit so she could see before being seen.

When she was as confident as she was going to get that the coast was clear, she exited the building.

Making a beeline for the car, she walked fast, but forced herself to not break into a run. That would only raise suspicion. She couldn't look as if she was fleeing, even if that was exactly what she was doing.

Hands shaking, she opened the rear passenger

side door. She tossed the bags onto the floor and strapped the baby into the car seat in the back, realizing if Tito got a look inside her car he'd see the telltale car seat and know what she had been hiding from him for the better part of the past year. A pregnancy. A baby.

She'd need to remove all evidence.

It would be okay. She'd take the seat out of the car when she got to the club. Whoever watched Lola for her would need the seat anyway.

Confident with that plan she slipped behind the wheel, checking the rearview mirror as she slid the key inside.

Memories of last night's car trouble hit her and she went cold with fear. Holding her breath, she turned the key in the ignition.

This time, it started right up.

Thank God for her unlikely guardian angel—Rocky, the bearded man from the bar. Whatever he'd done under the hood last night still held. She'd have to thank him one more time if she ever saw him again.

If she made it out of this thing alive.

Feeling sick to her stomach, and not because she'd never gotten to eat this morning, she pulled the car out of the space. She wouldn't feel better until this block was far behind her.

The club wasn't far, but it felt like an eternity to get there.

Lola, of course, fell asleep. Not a surprise. She had a full belly and a ride in the car always put her out like a light.

Thank goodness for that. Isabel was having

enough trouble figuring out what to do without having the baby screaming.

She slowed as she approached the turn into the lot for the club and eyed the few vehicles parked there, trying to determine if it was safe to pull in.

The presence of the big truck she'd seen Rocky go to last night surprised her.

Was he back there already? The guy had a problem if he was.

In the daylight she could see the truck more clearly, right down to the US NAVY bumper sticker.

Addiction to strip joints or not, it might be a good thing if he was here. She remembered how big he was. How capable under the hood. And with military training, he'd be handy to have around if the worst happened and Tito had followed her here.

That fear had her pulling past the club. She glanced in the rearview mirror and tried to determine if she was being tailed.

It always seemed so easy for the characters on TV to know when they were being followed, but in real life? Not so much.

Determined to be cautious, Isabel decided to drive around a little while and then circle back.

Better to be safe than sorry.

CHAPTER FOUR

Rocky emerged from the bathroom in his room in the bachelor barracks a tad hung over but at least he was feeling a little more awake after showering.

Too many beers, and two ill-advised shots of whisky last night, had him staying at the club later than he'd intended.

The whisky hadn't been all his fault. He'd bought a couple of shots for Jasmine and a gentleman never let a lady drink alone.

Whatever the reasons, it had resulted in him waking up late today. But if no shit hit the fan in the terrorist world that would require his team's immediate attention, he had a well-earned day off.

Now all he needed was his truck so he could get on with enjoying the day.

His vehicle, unfortunately, was still parked at the club where he'd left it last night.

Even if he could have driven home safely,

driving through the gate on base with alcohol on his breath would be a good way to fuck up his career. Elite SEAL or not, command took that shit seriously.

So step one, get his truck. Step two, figure out what to do with his day.

The bachelor-occupied housing on base was cheap and pretty nice as far as these things went, but no way was he spending his day off inside in a space that consisted of two small rooms sporting two windows total.

Nope, not Rocky's idea of fun.

Brody and Mack were both away for the weekend, but with any luck, Thom was around. And he was conveniently located in the same building.

After shoving his feet into sneakers, Rocky pocketed his keys and headed out. One flight down the stairs and he was knocking on Thom's door.

Thom answered with his cell phone pressed to one ear and motioned with his free hand for Rocky to come in as he spoke. "Bag of ice. Got it. Anything else?"

After a moment during which Rocky closed the door behind him and had time to wonder who in the world Thom was talking to about ice, Thom nodded. "Okay. See you in a few."

Once Thom had disconnected the call he turned to Rocky. "Hey, you got plans for the day?"

"Nope, not really. Why? What's happening?"

"Rick's throwing some stuff on the grill at his place. Jon is gonna be there. Grant might stop by and supposedly Chris and Brody are on the road back from Alabama and should be there by dinnertime."

"You sure it's okay if I come?" Rocky knew Rick through the other guys, but they weren't especially close.

Not like how friendly Rick was with the Cassidys and Thom since they'd all been on the same team together.

Thom's dark brows drew low in a frown. "Of course. It's fine. Rick's parties are always open door."

"All right. If you say so."

"Dude, definitely. The more the merrier."

He'd have preferred to hear that from Rick himself but he'd have to trust Thom.

Rocky nodded. "Okay. I'll pick up some beer to go along with your ice."

"Then he'll be even happier you're there." Thom grinned.

"Good. It's a plan. Which brings me to the reason I stopped by. Can you drop me at my truck on the way?"

"Sure thing. Where is it?"

"The strip club right outside the gate."

Thom laughed. "All right."

"What's so funny? I would've invited you but now that Ginny keeps your balls locked up in Connecticut, I figured you wouldn't be allowed to come."

Thom cocked a brow. "You want to walk to your truck?"

Though Rocky felt his statement had been true, he decided to back off any further comments about Thom being pussy whipped. "No."

"Didn't think so."

"So when are we leaving?" Rocky asked.

"When are you ready to go?"

He was as ready as he was going to get. He'd shoved some breakfast in his mouth before he'd showered. He had his keys and his wallet. He was dressed good enough for a barbecue.

Rocky lifted one shoulder. "Now."

"Okay. Let's go. We can stop at the commissary on the way off base, and then grab your truck and you can follow me to Rick's place."

"Sounds good." Rocky was all about being agreeable.

He could get his truck without having to call a cab and now he had plans for the day. Life was good.

That was reaffirmed when Thom pulled his SUV into the lot of the strip club and Rocky saw his parked truck, safe and sound right where he'd left it.

Surprisingly, there were quite a few other vehicles already parked there. He glanced at his watch and realized it was noon.

The club was open for another day and he had no doubt there were already dancers on the stage. Another day, another dollar bill shoved in their G-strings. The free enterprise system at work. It was enough to warm any red-blooded American male's heart.

With a promise to follow Thom, Rocky fished his keys out of his pocket and headed around to the driver's side of his truck.

Rick's house wasn't too far from the base so a short while later Rocky slowed behind Thom's

SUV as he pulled up along the curb in front of a small house sporting a neatly trimmed lawn.

With Thom toting the twenty-pound bag of ice and Rocky holding a case of beer, Thom hit the doorbell.

"I got it!" The sound of Rick's booming voice came through the door shortly before it whipped open to expose the man himself. "Hey. Come on in."

When Rick stepped back Thom asked, "Where do you want the ice?"

"Cooler is on the back deck. Beer can go in there too." Rick nodded to Rocky. "Good to see you, man. Glad you could make it."

"Thanks for having me."

"Not a problem. The more the merrier."

Thom shot Rocky a cocky glance that clearly said *I told you so* as Rick closed the door behind them.

Rocky rolled his eyes and followed Rick and Thom through the living room. They passed the kitchen on the way to the sliding glass door in the back of the house.

"Ladies." Thom nodded to the three women on the other side of the kitchen island as they passed.

"Hey, Thom." A blonde called out the greeting as they passed.

As Rick went ahead to open the door, Thom stopped and leaned close to Rocky. "Did you see who was in the kitchen?"

Rocky paused too. "You mean the blonde who said hello?"

"No, that was Rick's sister Darci. She's dating

Chris Cassidy. And the brunette next to her was Jon's girl Ali, but Sierra Cox is here. You know, the actress."

"Really? What's she doing here?"

"She's Rick's girlfriend."

Rocky frowned as he vaguely remembered Brody mentioning something about Rick and some actress. He supposed he didn't believe it then, but if she was in the kitchen with Rick's sister it must be true.

It still didn't explain the hows and whys of the situation. "How the fuck did he land her?"

"I guess taking a bullet for a woman has its benefits." Thom laughed.

Rocky had to agree as they moved toward the open door where Rick was waiting for them on the deck.

Outside, Rocky could see that while the women all seemed to be in the kitchen, the men had settled in on the deck by the beer.

Jon was already there, leaning against the railing with a longneck in his hand.

"We have arrived and we brought provisions." Thom dropped the bag of ice on the deck and reached to open the lid on a big blue cooler.

Rocky set the beer down and turned to Jon, who stepped forward to shake hands. "Good to see you again."

Rocky snorted. "Good to see you on US soil this time."

Jon grinned. "That too."

Not long ago Rocky's SEAL team had spent some time with Jon's company, GAPS, in Nigeria.

The military was turning more and more to using private contractors for consulting and extra manpower.

Rick let out a huff. "I can't believe I missed that job."

Jon cocked one dark brow. "If I remember correctly you were in New York, no doubt staying at some fancy hotel and working security for People Magazine's Sexiest Woman on Earth, so no complaining."

"Yeah. While we were sweating our balls off in the Sambisa Forest. You forget how hot Africa is?" Thom asked.

"I remember."

Rocky had to laugh as Rick continued to scowl and look unhappy about missing the op. "I gotta agree with them, Rick. You get no sympathy. We were fighting Boko Haram and frigging snakes at the same time. I can tell you one thing, if I'm gonna be killed in action, it better not be from a damn snakebite."

Thom jumped up from his knees where he'd been kneeling to load the beer and ice in the cooler. "Oh my God. Rick, you have to picture this. There are four of us, in position, on our stomachs sighting the path out of the target's camp with our rifles . . ."

Shaking his head at Thom's retelling of the snake story for what had to be the tenth time, Rocky kneeled down and took over arranging the beer and ice in the cooler.

When it was packed, he popped the top on one for himself and settled into a chair as Thom finished the tale and they all had a good laugh at Rocky's expense over how he'd been afraid of a snake.

Only then could Rocky finally get on with enjoying the day.

"So what did we miss around here while we've been gone?" Thom asked Rick.

It was a good question. They'd been away more than they'd been home this year.

"The big guy here made a lot of changes actually." Rick hooked a thumb in Jon's direction. "Did you hear he asked Ali to move in with him?"

Thom's eyes widened. "No. He didn't mention it. Wow, dude, are there wedding bells in your future?"

Jon glanced at the door of the house and then back to Thom. "Don't rush things, okay? Her lease was up and the landlord was going to hike the rent up ridiculously high. It seemed practical for her to move in with me."

"So romantic." Rick laughed. "You'll notice, Rocky, that Jon's not one to do anything fast. Took him over a year to finally rent an office for GAPS and he still won't hire a secretary."

Jon rolled his eyes. "I know you and Zane have visions of us hiring some James Bond-worthy Miss Moneypenny to answer the phone, but it's not gonna happen. We also don't have Q and all his toys and none of you are getting a rocket-fueled BMW either. GAPS is a private contractor. Not MI6."

Rick scowled. "I know that but I really do think we need a plane. Chris has his pilot's license. Think of all the money you'd save on flying commercial."

"Sure. Why don't we get a CH-53 too? That way

we won't have to bother the Marines when we need a helo." Jon snorted. "And what do you care anyway? Sierra has you all sewn up as her head of security. When are you going to be available to work a job with GAPS again?"

"Personally, I think a Blackhawk is more versatile than a Super Stallion." Thom always was one to stir the pot.

Ignoring Thom's unsolicited comment, Rick frowned at Jon. "I'm gonna work more jobs with you. I'll have time between her movies. And I saw you ordered company logo shirts. I want one. An extra-large, please."

Jon blew out a derogatory sounding snort. "I didn't order those shirts. Zane did. I'm lucky I talked him out of the logo golf balls."

Rocky watched the exchange between the two men, happy all he had to do was take orders from his command, because judging by this conversation leaving the military and starting a private company hadn't been without its challenges for Jon.

Thom glanced sideways at Rocky. "Makes the Navy not seem all that bad, huh?"

Rocky laughed that Thom had been thinking the same thing he had. "You ain't kidding."

The glass door sliding open had Rocky's attention shifting to the house just as Darci popped her head out. "The chili is hot so anytime you want some, just go grab it from the stove."

"Thanks, Darci." Rick turned back to the guys. "I figure I'll throw the burgers and dogs on the grill in a couple of hours. Brody and Chris should be here before dark."

The distant sound of the doorbell ringing filtered out to the deck. Rick leaned forward in his chair and peered through the sliding glass door. “Who the hell could that be? Chris and Brody couldn’t be back in town yet and everybody else is already here.”

Jon shrugged. “Maybe Darci or Ali asked somebody from work.”

“Or maybe it’s Grant. You said you called him too, right?” Thom reminded Rick.

“Yeah, I did. But he was having trouble getting the wife onboard with the plan and said he probably wouldn’t make it.” Rick hoisted his large frame from the chair and stood. “I guess we’ll find out soon enough.”

“Rick!” Darci’s shout came from inside the house. “Get in here. Now!”

“What the hell is wrong with her?” Rick drew his brows low as he moved to open the door.

Rocky watched Rick go into the house, curious but not enough to get out of his chair. It seemed the other guys felt the same. Jon and Thom stayed put as well.

“What the hell?” That exclamation from Rick propelled the men into action. They all stood at once.

Jon was the first to get to the door. He stopped dead, blocking Thom and Rocky’s entry and their view.

“Holy shit. Whose is that?” At Jon’s question, Rocky couldn’t take it any longer.

He edged past the blockage and finally got a look around Jon at what all the cursing was about.

A car seat containing a baby sat in the center of

the dining room table. And surrounding the table were three very unhappy looking women.

Darci crossed her arms. "That's exactly what I'd like to know."

"Zane's maybe?" Rick lifted one shoulder. "He was a real dog before he got together with Missy."

The usually lovely and perfectly composed Sierra Cox, at least when he'd seen her on television, didn't look as if she was buying it.

"There's one problem with that theory. Your friend Zane doesn't live here," Sierra pointed out.

Darci nodded. "But you do, Rick."

Uh oh. It looked like Rick was in big trouble as both his girlfriend and his sister presented a united front against him.

Rick stood his ground and leveled a gaze on his girlfriend. "The problem with that circumstantial evidence is that before you I lived like a monk. So no, it's not mine if that's what you're both insinuating."

Darci glanced at Sierra. "That is true. He like never dated. Ever."

Rick scowled. "Thanks, sis. And might I remind you that you live here too? Maybe this is about you."

Darci lifted a brow. "I think I'd know if I had a baby, Rick."

"I didn't mean you. I'm talking about Chris."

Rocky watched wide-eyed as Rick threw Chris Cassidy, Darci's boyfriend, under the bus. He'd worked with Chris on that op in Nigeria. He was a good man and all evidence indicated he'd been a good SEAL before he'd retired and joined Jon's team on GAPS.

Darci visibly paled at her brother's accusation.

Rocky didn't feel right standing by silently. If Chris's friends and former teammates didn't defend him, he would. "Hey, now. Let's not make any assumptions. Chris isn't here to defend himself."

Meanwhile the baby, already squirming in the seat, began to wail. The noise only seemed to ramp up the tension in the room.

No one made a move toward the baby and the screaming continued. It probably went on for less than a minute but it felt like an eternity.

A crying baby was one of those sounds that grated on the nerves pretty fast.

Finally Jon's girlfriend Ali stepped forward. "For goodness sake. If no one is going to pick up the poor child, I will."

Instinct and training kicked in for Rocky. A terrorist wouldn't think twice about wiring a baby seat to explode. He took one step forward. "No!"

Almost simultaneously, Jon shouted, "Ali, don't!"

Rick ran for Sierra and shoved both her and Darci into the kitchen as Thom dropped to the floor and shielded his head with his forearms.

All of them had to be thinking the same thing. As SEALs they'd all been in too many hellholes in the world where US forces would go to investigate a body or help what appeared to be a person in need, only to be blown to bits when they got close.

Heart pounding, Rocky watched Ali release the buckle and slide her hands beneath the crying baby's arms.

The whole scene seemed to move in slow motion. She lifted the baby from the car seat before Jon got to her.

Seconds ticked by in the surreal way they do when adrenaline is pounding through the bloodstream during a crisis. But the explosion never came.

Ali frowned at Jon. "What's wrong with you?"

"Get into the other room." Jon shoved Ali and the baby toward the kitchen doorway, where Rick had already pushed Sierra and Darci.

Once she was clear of the immediate area, Jon bent low to peer beneath the car seat on the table. Thom hoisted himself off the floor as Rocky stepped forward to join Jon in examining the seat.

Sad but true, the innocent-looking baby seat could be wired with explosives. The fact they were standing in Rick's dining room in Virginia in the good old United States didn't matter. ISIS was here in America. That was a proven fact.

"What do you think?" Rocky asked Jon.

"Hell if I know." Jon glanced up at Thom. "Get over here. You have kids. You're the only one who knows what this thing is supposed to look like."

Thom stepped forward and bent low too, the three of them squinting at a contraption that looked innocuous enough—to a person who hadn't spent the last decade of their life searching for threats around every turn and beneath every rock.

Darci peeked past Rick's bulk as he blocked the women in the kitchen. "You guys are ridiculous."

Rick scowled. "Darci, be quiet and let us figure out what's going on."

"How about you read that note that fell out of the blanket when Ali picked up the baby? Maybe it will give you men folk a clue while us helpless women hide in the kitchen."

Darci's statement about a note had Rocky tearing his gaze away from the seat. He searched the area beneath the table. Sure enough a paper was resting on the carpet by Jon's feet.

Jon bent to pick it up. He lifted a brow and then glanced up. "Rocky?"

"Yeah?"

"It seems this delivery is for you."

Rocky's eyes flew wide. "What?"

Thom leaned closer to Jon to inspect the paper. "Yup. Says Rocky right there on it, plain as day. Dude, what have you been doing?"

"Nothing. I've been out of the country with you for most of the last seven months." His mind spun with all the places he'd been in that time.

"And it takes nine months to make a baby, so . . ." Rick tipped his head to the side and let that idea dangle in the air as Rocky's world tilted and spun.

Thom glanced at Ali, who'd finally quieted the baby and had come back to hover on the edge of the room. "And by the looks of that baby, she's a few months old. So the question remains, what were you doing about a year ago?"

Rocky could barely remember this morning, never mind what he was doing last year. Still, a feeling of doom settled in his stomach.

A baby? What the fuck? Given how little free time he had there hadn't been a whole lot of women in his life, but even so he'd always been careful.

"Why don't you stop thinking so hard and just read the note?" Jon extended the hand holding the fateful piece of paper that could change Rocky's whole future.

With his chest so tight he could barely draw breath he took it. He'd faced bullets with less fear than he felt opening that folded paper.

His gaze shot past the page filled with neat writing, to the bottom and the signature. *Isabel.*

Why did that name sound familiar?

Shit. Was this kid his?

He forced his eyes to go back to the top, cleared his throat and began to read aloud. "Rocky. We met last night at the strip club when you helped me with my car."

Met last night? That hint jogged his hazy memory. He remembered Isabel and the car, but what did that have to do with this baby? As far as he could recall he'd never met her before last night.

Not yet relieved of the fear that this baby might be his somehow, he forced himself to continue reading.

"You seem like a man I can trust. I beg you for your help in keeping my daughter Lola safe. I will come for her when I can. Until then please do not report anything to the police or they will take her from me. Please. Keeping her a secret is more important than I can say, for reasons I can't tell you. The things she will need are in the bags I am leaving with her. I owe you my life and hers. Isabel."

Rocky glanced up to find the room full of stunned people watching him.

"Shit." Rick shook his head. "I have so many questions I don't know where to start."

"Then I'll start. Was there a bag outside?" Jon asked Darci.

"I don't know. I was so shocked by the baby, I didn't notice. I just grabbed the handle and carried her in."

"I'll go check." Jon moved toward the front door as Rocky began to feel a little unsteady on his feet.

He glanced at the baby, wrapped in a pink blanket and still in Ali's arms.

What the hell was he going to do with a baby? And how long was Isabel going to take to retrieve her?

Hours? Days? Any longer and this was going to be a big problem.

For one thing, he could get recalled on an hour's notice. But more than that, he wasn't allowed to have any overnight visitors in the barracks. Not guys. Not girls. And certainly not a three-month old baby who would make her presence known with every unhappy yowl.

"I can't bring her back to the barracks. And I don't know shit about babies." Rocky looked at Thom. "You're going to have to take her."

"Me? What the fuck am I supposed to do with her? I'm in the barracks just like you are."

"Relax. Rocky, you can stay here with her until we figure this thing out."

He raised his eyes to Darci at her kind offer. "Really? That'd be okay?"

"Of course. Just don't expect me to take care of her. I don't know anything about babies either."

Rocky shifted his gaze to Thom, hoping his helpless expression would sway the man. "Will you stay with me?"

"I guess. If that's all right." Thom glanced at Darci and Rick.

"Sure." Rick nodded. "We'll figure something out. Wouldn't be the first time you crashed on my sofa."

"I can sleep at Chris's place and Rocky and Thom can have my room. You two and Rick, on babysitting duty." Darci shook her head. "Kind of sorry I won't be here to see it."

"Me too." Sierra smiled.

"You're not staying here with us?" Rick's eyes widened.

"I have a suite at the Ritz, so no." Sierra looked every bit the diva as Rick pouted and Rocky's head spun.

He and Thom and the baby, bunking together in Darci's room in Rick's house. The situation got weirder by the moment.

"Maybe this Isabel will be back soon and no one will have to stay," Ali offered.

Jon returned to the dining room and dumped an overstuffed bag onto the table. In his other hand he held a plastic bag that was leaking water onto the carpet.

"Judging by the amount of stuff she packed for the kid she's not planning to be back today." He turned toward the kitchen, catching the dripping liquid from the bag in his hand. "There are four bottles in here. Thom, how long before we run out of stuff to feed her?"

Thom’s eyes widened. “It’s been a long time since my kids were that age. And to be honest, I was away for a lot of that time. Probably why I’m divorced today but still, I’m sorry but I’m not really sure.”

“We’ll search on the internet about what she’s supposed to be eating and then go out and buy what we need when we run out.” Darci was already opening a laptop she’d grabbed from somewhere.

Rocky was in a daze of shock but clarity was starting to take over again. There was something productive he could do, and it entailed more than researching feeding a baby.

He stood. “I know she left this baby for me, but if somebody could just watch her for a little bit, maybe I can figure out what the hell is going on.”

“How do you intend to do that?” Rick asked.

“I know what she looks like. What car she drives. Hopefully I can track down Isabel or at least question her coworkers. She works at the strip club. I can ask around there. Hell, maybe she’s there working now.”

Jon nodded. “That’s a good plan. One of us should go with you. In case there’s trouble.”

“I’ll go.” Rick stepped forward.

At the same time, Thom said, “I’m coming.”

“Oh no. All of you men are not leaving us here to babysit.” Ali cocked a brow as the men tried to flee.

“Yeah, especially since this website says a three-month old could need to eat every two to three hours. That’s just crazy. We’re going to run out of those bottles fast. Then we’ll have to buy formula, I guess." Darci turned her panicked focus to the only one among them with baby experience. "Thom, you can't go. I have no idea what I'm doing with a baby."

"I agree. He needs to stay." Sierra nodded.

"Besides, if there really is some sort of danger frightening enough that it compelled this woman to leave her baby on the doorstep of strangers just to keep her safe, don't you think we might need some protection here?" Darci crossed her arms while cocking a brow.

Jon drew in a breath. "They're right. Two go and two stay. Rocky obviously needs to go since he's the only one who knows what this woman looks like. Who do you want with you, Rocky?"

Rocky lifted his chin toward Jon. "You carrying?"

Jon tipped his head. "Always."

"Then you're with me." Confident in his decision, Rocky ignored Rick and Thom's twin scowls at being left behind with the females.

Rocky wasn't being unfair. He did have a reason for his choice. It made sense. This was Rick's house. If the shit hit the fan, he'd know how to best defend it. No doubt there was a gun safe in the house and he needed to be here to open it. And Thom was the only one among them blessed with children of his own, so he should be there too and make sure they didn't feed the kid the wrong stuff.

Rocky paused at the front door and glanced back. "We'll be back as soon as we can. I'll call when we know anything. And call us if Isabel shows up."

"We can only hope." Rick snorted.

"Good luck," Ali called after them.

Rocky had a feeling they were going to need it.

They were outside and heading for Rocky's truck when Jon paused for a second before continuing his stride across the lawn. "Don't look but I think our momma hasn't gone too far."

"What?" Rocky forced himself to glance at Jon and not at his surroundings.

"I caught movement across the street when I came outside for the diaper bag and now I just saw it again. Same spot. I'm willing to bet she's hanging around to make sure the baby is all right."

"So what do we do? Flush her out?" Rocky asked, his heart pounding as hard as if they were on a mission in hostile territory rather than trying to catch a young mother in the suburbs of Virginia.

"You and I are gonna get in your truck. We'll draw her attention while Thom and Rick sneak out the back."

"And grab her." Rocky drew in a breath at the thought.

She was going to be scared to death, but he didn't see how they had any other choice. They needed answers. More than that he needed to not be responsible for an infant. The Naval Special Warfare department didn't give SEALs time off for babysitting strangers' kids . . . not that he'd ever had occasion to ask.

He sighed. "All right."

Rocky clicked to unlock the truck as Jon pulled out his cell phone to fill Rick and Thom in on the situation.

CHAPTER FIVE

Isabel watched from behind a shrub on the corner as the two men came out of the house she'd followed Rocky to.

She recognized Rocky, the man she'd trusted on gut instinct alone to shelter her daughter. Next to him walked the guy who'd come outside before to grab the diaper bag and milk. She'd had to duck back fast before he saw her.

Good thing she'd hidden. He'd looked all around the house and up and down the street before going back inside with the bags.

She should have left immediately after ringing the doorbell, but she couldn't bring herself to.

Her baby was in that house, and as Rocky opened the door of his truck and climbed inside, along with the other dark-haired man, it was obvious he was leaving Lola behind.

It would be all right. The people inside had to be

Rocky's friends. If he trusted them with the baby she had to trust them too.

Even so, she'd stay around for a little while anyway. At least to make sure they'd done as she'd asked and didn't call the police.

Meanwhile there were a million things she should be doing. Emptying her apartment of anything that hinted at Lola's existence was prime among them.

She had no doubt Tito wouldn't think twice about breaking into her place if he found the apartment empty. And the moment he saw the baby things, he'd figure out why she'd left Miami—left him—so suddenly all those months ago.

Torn, she considered the options. Stay and watch to make sure the baby was all right. Or go and cover her trail and insure Lola would remain okay. Protecting her secret won out. It was time to go.

If the police were coming, Rocky would have stayed to talk to them. After all, his name had been on the note.

She had to believe the people in that house would care for her child until she could come back to get her.

When would that be?

That all depended on Tito. She needed a plan, but sanitizing the house came first.

Her car was parked nearby, on the side street of the corner where she now hid, out of view of the house.

She spun toward it, only to come face to face with two men who'd somehow managed to sneak up on her. Only putting the brakes on her momentum saved her from crashing directly into them.

"Um, sorry. Didn't hear you there. Excuse me. I need to go."

The bigger one, a blonde with a muscled torso like a brick wall, crossed his arms and lifted a brow. "And where's that?"

Her eyes widened. "To meet my boyfriend. He's uh waiting for me."

"Oh, is he now?"

Self preservation kicked in and she took a step back.

The other guy stepped forward. He was no less fit but a little less large. "Rick. Stop. You're upsetting her."

"Am I? Well, Thom, I was a little upset myself finding a baby on my stoop."

His words were like a punch to her gut. "You have Lola?"

Rick's eyes widened. "Yeah, we have Lola. What do you think? You left her at my door."

Thom scowled at Rick before he turned toward her. "Isabel. We're friends of Rocky's. Lola is fine. She's at the house with Rick's sister and our friends. We only want to talk."

She shook her head. "I can't talk. I have to go."

As she moved to leave in spite of the two men, a now familiar looking truck skidded to a stop, blocking her car in.

Fleeing was obviously going to be impossible. She couldn't drive away and if she ran, she had no doubt they'd catch her. She knew the type. These guys probably ran ten miles and lifted weights in the gym before most people got out of bed in the morning.

As Rocky got out of the truck with the other guy, she was surrounded and way outnumbered.

She sagged with a full body sigh. “Fine. I’ll talk to you but is there any way we can do it at my apartment?”

“Why?” The question came from Rocky in a soft tone that accompanied the hand he laid on her arm.

Near tears, she didn’t have any lies left. “Because if my ex gets there first and goes inside, there’s a good chance he’s going to come after me. And when he finds me, he’ll probably kill me and then take the baby.”

Her statement elicited a visual exchange between the four men.

Rocky drew in a breath that expanded his chest. She tried not to notice the swell but it was impossible, they stood so close. “Me and Jon will go with Isabel to her place. You two stay here.”

“Yeah. I want enough protection for the baby and the women in case she was followed. You need a weapon?” Rick asked Rocky.

The question had her glancing at Rocky and waiting for the answer.

“I’m good. Got it locked in the truck.”

She didn’t know whether to be relieved or scared that her escort had a weapon.

Tito and his crew were all usually armed to the teeth, with guns she suspected weren’t exactly legal. That should have been her first clue he wasn’t the ideal guy for her first serious boyfriend.

But bringing armed men to her apartment where

she expected Tito could show up at any moment was asking for trouble.

A shootout between these men and her ex was the last thing she wanted. But the thought of facing Tito alone was no better.

Rocky glanced at her. “Come on. Let’s go.”

“Okay. You can follow me to my apartment.”

“You can ride with us.” Rocky pressed a hand against her lower back.

Even through her shirt, she felt the heat. The strength. It gave her comfort even if he was in effect steering her away from her own car and toward his truck.

She was depending too much on a man who was a stranger to her. Trusting him to do what was best to protect her even though there was nothing concrete behind that trust. But here in a foreign country so many miles from everyone and everything she’d grown up knowing, she had no one else she could count on.

She’d trusted Tito once upon a time as well. That had been the worst decision of her life.

Glancing at these men around her, Rocky in particular, she was very aware of her track record with trusting the wrong men.

Was she repeating her mistake? Times four?

No, somehow she didn’t think so. These men seemed different. The cool precision with which they reacted to her fears over Tito and formed a plan spoke to practiced, calculated action, probably gained through military training if Rocky’s US NAVY bumper sticker was any indication.

“All right.” She glanced back at her car.

"Leave your car there for now. It's legally parked and far enough from the house it won't tip off anyone who's looking for you." Rick answered her unspoken question.

His reasoning made sense so she nodded. "Okay."

"You ready to go? Got everything you need?" Rocky asked.

Her cell was in her pocket. Her bag could stay in the car. The keys were clutched in her hand. The apartment key was on the same key ring as the car key. She clicked to engage the automatic locks.

"Yes. I'm ready." She only wished that statement were true.

Inside the cab of the truck, sandwiched between Rocky and Jon's bulk, mixed feelings ricocheted through her. She gave Rocky her address and he took off in the direction of her apartment.

She was trapped, unable to get out either door past the men. But she was also sheltered. Protected by their bodies, not to mention their weapons, which they'd both checked the moment they'd gotten into the vehicle.

"Want to fill us in on what we're walking into? Why your ex wants to kill you?" Jon asked in an even tone that belied the question.

The answer to that was no, she really didn't want to tell them anything just as she didn't want to face it herself, but she'd run out of options.

"I kind of left without saying goodbye." Her elusive statement was met with silence. They were obviously waiting for her to elaborate. She drew in a deep breath and forged ahead. "I never told him I was pregnant. He knows nothing about Lola."

"He's the father?" Rocky asked.

"Yes, he's the father." It was a kneejerk reaction, her getting insulted by the question even though she probably had no right to be.

How could these men know she'd been a virgin when she'd met Tito? That he was still the one and only man she'd ever been intimate with.

"What's this guy's full name?" Jon asked.

"Tito Perez."

"Why did you leave?" Rocky asked.

"And where did you leave from?" In the tag team questioning, it was Jon's turn to have a go.

"Miami. I was in the final year of university there. I left because he . . ." She had to swallow and steady herself before continuing, "because he was not a very nice man."

Out of her peripheral vision she saw Jon typing on his cell phone.

At the same time, Rocky asked, "Care to elaborate on that?"

She was feeling a bit ganged up on as they fired questions at her, but she supposed there were a lot of things they should know considering there was a very real chance they could come face to face with Tito at her apartment.

Like it or not, they were all in this together now.

She swallowed and steeled herself for the revelation. "He was involved in bad stuff with bad men. And he didn't treat me right."

When she'd tried to break up with him, he'd slapped her around so badly she'd had to go to the campus infirmary and pretend she'd fallen down the stairs.

"Why didn't you just go to the police in Miami?"

"He would have hurt me—or worse." She had no doubt in her mind about that. "I had to disappear. Leave the state before he figured out I was pregnant. And now I have to hide all evidence that Lola exists before he sees it and figures out she's his."

She had two lives to worry about now.

Rocky glanced in her direction. "The police can protect you."

"You don't know how powerful he is. He has connections."

Jon shook his head. "Maybe he had connections in Miami. We're in Virginia now. You'd be safe contacting the authorities here."

She drew in a breath. This was the part where she really had to trust these men.

"There's something else." Both men turned to look at her. She swallowed and continued, "I'm Cuban and my student visa is no longer valid because I left school. If I'm not a full time student, I'm here illegally."

Rocky pursed his lips and nodded. "Okay. We deal with one problem at a time. First, we clean out your apartment and figure out what to do about good old Tito."

"And then?" she asked.

He shot her a glance. "What about the concept of dealing with one problem at a time didn't you understand?"

She scowled. "Don't try and tell me you guys don't plan things out, down to the last detail. I don't believe it."

On the other side of her, Jon laughed. "She's got you there. But as much as we do like to plan, we also know there are plenty of times the situation will go sideways. Then we ditch the plan and have to think on our feet."

Her expression must have appeared less than confident after his revelation.

Rocky shot her a smile. "Don't worry. We're very good on our feet."

As the heat of his thigh pressed against hers from the tight confines of the truck's bench seat, she had to think he was probably good everywhere.

And that right there was proof she suffered from the damsel in distress syndrome. Wanting to be saved. Waiting for her knight in shining armor to ride in on a white charger—or pick-up truck as the case may be.

Her psych teacher would have had a field day analyzing that.

Maybe she was just noticing Rocky's muscular thigh straining the denim of his jeans because she hadn't had sex in a year. Even though Tito had been her first—and that relationship had been spectacularly bad—it didn't mean she was ready for him to be the last.

If she lived through this she would get on with her life. Get her degree, somehow, somewhere. Meet men and date again. Learn to trust again, and maybe even fall in love.

The fact she was sitting between these two men now proved she could still find the strength to put her trust in someone, in spite of the devastating results of the last time she'd done so.

There was hope.

As Rocky swung the truck onto her block and her heart pounded as she visually swept the street looking for trouble, she had to believe that. There would be hope for tomorrow. She just had to get through today.

"That's my building. On the right."

Rocky slowed the truck to a stop along the curb and threw the gear shift into Park. He scanned the street in front of them and behind them before turning his attention to her. "You ready to go in?"

Jon was already out of the truck and conducting a visual search of his own.

Isabel nodded. It was obvious she had to be ready. She had no choice.

CHAPTER SIX

Rocky tracked Isabel's progress as she bounced around the apartment. Nervous energy or just plain fear had sent her into perpetual motion.

At one point she was literally turning in circles trying to do everything at once and instead getting nothing at all done.

"Hey." He grabbed her arm as she strode past where he stood keeping an eye on the street through the window. He felt her shaking as she spun toward him, eyes wide.

"Yeah?"

"You can slow down. We have time."

"No, I can't. We have to get out of here."

"Yeah, but when you rush, you make mistakes. Forget things."

Ten minutes either way wouldn't make a difference. And much more of this frenzy and she'd work herself into being even more of a mess.

Her manic, frantic, not to mention messy packing was starting to get to him. It shouldn't. He'd been trained for worse than the possibility of an ex-boyfriend knocking on the door.

Hell, he'd faced men ten times worse than a thug from Miami who liked to knock around a woman half his size.

In fact, Rocky kind of hoped this Tito did show up while he was there. He'd enjoy teaching him what it felt like to be on the receiving end of a fist. What it felt like to fight fair on a level playing field against an equal opponent.

Okay, maybe not *quite* equal. Rocky had no doubt he could kick this Tito's ass.

But at the moment, he had a bigger battle to win—the one being waged by Isabel's panic as it warred with her ability to concentrate.

"You're safe as long as you're with Jon and me. Even if Tito shows up, you're safe. I swear." He grinned and tried to lighten the mood. "And I'm first-generation American, born and raised in a strict Italian-Catholic household so you know you can trust me since I don't swear lightly."

She drew in a deep breath, expanding her chest until her tits strained the fabric of her shirt. His grandmother and mother would have both taken a wooden spoon to him if they'd been there to see him noticing her chest.

He shouldn't be looking, but he couldn't help it. The woman was built. That was to be expected he supposed. She did work at the strip club.

At the moment he couldn't remember if he'd ever seen her dance. Damn his bad memory.

Isabel shook her head. “You don’t know what he’s like.”

Back to the baby-daddy. Rocky had happily pushed him out of his mind but here he was, back again.

“It doesn’t matter. We’re prepared. If he shows up here we’ll deal with him.”

“And what about after I’m out of here? Where do I go? Where do I take Lola that he won’t find us again? I moved us here after I had Lola thinking it would be safer to get out of the state where I had her, but it’s obvious I wasn’t careful enough since he found me.” Her eyes filled with tears. “I’m scared.”

Her final words were spoken so softly they were barely a whisper but he heard them. Hell, he felt the fear radiating off her.

“We’ll figure it out.” He squeezed her arm and then dropped his hold. “Finish your packing. Let me know if you need help with anything heavy.”

“I’ll be fine. I moved in here alone.” She shrugged and turned toward the bedroom, and he bit back a curse.

She shouldn’t have had to move in alone. Just like she shouldn’t have had to flee her life in Miami. Certainly not while pregnant, or after she had an infant to care for.

A text from Jon lit Rocky’s cell. He was on his way back into the apartment after doing a walk around the building. Good. They needed to talk.

The door opened and Rocky tipped a chin in his direction. “Glad you’re back.”

Jon moved closer, the expression on his face

grim. "Wish I was as glad about what I have to report."

He'd kept his voice low, but even so, Rocky glanced at the bedroom door to make sure Isabel wasn't in hearing distance before he asked, "What have you got?"

"I'd texted Rick the guy's name and last known residence." Jon blew out a long slow breath. "Your girl sure picked a winner of a boyfriend."

Rocky pushed past the fact that Isabel wasn't his girl—though he wouldn't exactly hate it if she was—and moved on to the more pertinent topic. "What's he into?"

"Everything. Illegal arms. Drugs. Typical mob stuff."

"Wonderful." Shaking his head, Rocky blew out a loud breath filled with frustration. "She's scared, man."

"Yeah, I know. Watching us come in here as if we were breaching an insurgent hideout probably didn't help."

Rocky snorted. "Yeah, no shit."

With decades of training and operations between them, he and Jon had fallen easily into full tactical mode. Flanking the doorway, they'd cleared the apartment with guns drawn. All while Isabel watched, visibly shaken.

"We need to keep her with us." He glanced up at Jon. "Sorry. She's not your responsibility. I meant *I* need to keep her with me. Somewhere safe."

Rocky had made the decision. He just hadn't figured out the logistics yet.

The fact remained he lived in the bachelor

barracks. What his room lacked in space, it made up for in an overabundance of rules particularly pertaining to visitors of the opposite sex.

"How long have you known her?" Jon asked.

"I met her last night in the parking lot of the club. Her car was acting up. I took a look under the hood."

"Just under the hood of the car? Nothing else?"

Rocky drew his brows low at the unspoken insinuation. "I fixed a loose wire and she drove away."

"Then she's not exactly your responsibility either."

Sometimes Jon could be too logical, almost to the point of being cold. Unfeeling. It might make for a good businessman and team leader, but Rocky tended to live more by his emotions.

It had served him well so far. He was still alive, wasn't he? More than once, a good rush of anger had given him the push he needed to survive. It was sometimes that extra burst of adrenaline that put the winner over the top.

"I'm protecting her." Rocky's tone left no room for debate.

"Okay." Jon dipped his head in a nod of acceptance.

Even with as determined as he was, logic began to creep in. Rocky huffed out a breath. "What the fuck am I gonna do about her if I get called in? I could be out of the country for months."

"Yeah, you could."

He couldn't ask them to protect her if he deployed. It was bad enough he might have to impose on Rick or Jon to put her and the baby up for the night. Him too, since he wasn't leaving her alone.

Maybe for tonight he could rent her a room at the hotel on the base. She and the baby would be allowed to stay there as long as he booked the room. She'd be safer on base than at a hotel out in town.

That solved the immediate issue of where to stash her and Lola. He could figure the rest out later.

"There's something else."

There was Jon again, splashing cold water on his plans right after he'd settled everything in his mind.

"Yeah?"

"Rick called Zane about her immigration issue."

Shit. He'd forgotten that part. She was in the country with an invalid student visa since she was no longer a student. But what the hell did Jon's partner in GAPS have to do with any of that. "Zane? Why?"

"He's got connections in the Capitol. I thought he might have some insight, if not be able to pull some strings."

"And?"

"He thinks it's possible he can put her in touch with the proper people to get it straightened out given the circumstances, but it's going to take time. Until she speaks with an immigration lawyer, his instinct is for her to lay low."

"Meaning don't go to the police even if there is a mobster from Miami after her?"

"Yeah. I have to say I agree with him. The last thing we need is some cop playing things by the book, contacting immigration and getting her deported to Cuba. We can protect her while she's here. Not once she's there."

One word Jon spoke stuck out for Rocky. He decided to comment on it. "We?"

"Of course. I'm not gonna abandon her. Or you either if you insist on being the hero. GAPS has done well this year. We can spare a little manpower for some pro bono work."

"Thanks." A little choked up at the generosity, Rocky didn't know what else to say.

"No problem. We got your six." Jon grinned.

If that didn't happen to be the GAPS company motto, the one currently embroidered beneath the logo on the front of Jon's black shirt, the sentiment might have meant more.

But hell, at the moment he'd take what he could get.

CHAPTER SEVEN

Her whole life—what remained of it anyway—was shoved in the bed of the pick-up truck belonging to a man she'd known for less than a full day.

As much of her and Lola's clothing as would fit was inside the only two suitcases she owned. The rest of their combined belongings were stashed in trash bags—a quick fix for lack of a better option.

She'd been planning to only remove evidence of Lola's existence, but she'd been overruled. The two men with her, who seemed to operate like this trip to her apartment was a mission against an enemy army, had suggested very strongly that she clean out the apartment completely.

Since they were offering up Rocky's truck and their manpower to help her, she really couldn't argue. She could sense they weren't going to budge on their plan.

So even though the rent was paid through the end of next month, her two-room furnished apartment was empty of anything from her time there. She'd be lying if she didn't admit that was extremely depressing.

In spite of that grim reality, Isabel was grateful for the help. Rocky's generosity had saved her in so many ways in such a short time, from fixing her car last night, to taking in Lola today, to hauling her stuff now.

She could never even begin to repay him or his friends for the help she'd already accepted from them, and this ordeal wasn't over yet. Accepting something she didn't deserve didn't come easily to her. Doing so stung the pride instilled in her over a lifetime of being raised by a strong-willed grandmother in Cuba who stood on her own two feet in spite of overwhelming odds.

But Isabel had no choice.

Rocky steered the truck off the highway and onto a street she recognized. They were almost to his friend's house. She'd be reunited with her daughter soon.

He glanced past her and to Jon. "I figure we'll ask Rick if we can unload everything into the garage."

Jon nodded. "Good plan. Then she can sort it out inside."

"Yup. That's what I'm thinking. Behind closed doors and out of view of the street." Rocky finally switched his focus to her. "Pull out anything you'll need for the next couple of days. Hopefully Rick and his sister will let you keep the rest here for the duration. There's not a whole lot. If it's a problem keeping it here, I'll bring it over to my storage unit."

Jon shook his head. "It shouldn't be a problem. Rick never puts his truck in the garage. He and his sister shouldn't mind."

Her stuff was going to live in the garage of the house belonging to the big scary blonde guy and his sister? Why would two people she didn't know go out of their way to help a stranger?

That seemed odd to her but it was far from her biggest concern. There were so many more baffling things.

Isabel watched the men talking over her like this was a tennis match and she was the net.

"You look like you have questions about the plan, so ask." Rocky must have seen her frown.

She raised her eyes to meet his golden brown gaze. "I'm just confused. I didn't realize we had a plan."

At least no plan past getting her stuff out of the apartment and out of sight before Tito spotted them.

Rocky grinned. "We always have a plan.

"Okay." She sounded about as skeptical as she felt.

"You don't believe me that we have one, do you?"

"I do . . . I guess. What is it?" She didn't want to insult him but she couldn't exactly lie either.

"First, we'll ask Rick about leaving your things here."

"Why?"

"Because I got nowhere secure to lock up my

truck with all your stuff exposed in the bed. Aside from the chance someone could steal your shit, I don't want to risk leaving all the things we're trying to hide from your ex out in the open for him to find."

She didn't love that idea but it made sense, at least.

"Yup." Jon tipped his head in agreement with Rocky. "On top of that, we were parked in front of your apartment for a long time. I don't think we were followed but we can't risk the vehicle being spotted and recognized. We need to unload and then move the truck away from the house so it doesn't lead anyone right here to you."

Followed? This was feeling more and more like a television cop show than her shambles of a life.

If it were a show, everything would be wrapped up neatly within the forty minutes of the program, not counting commercial breaks.

Wouldn't that be nice?

Unfortunately this was very real, and she had another real concern to inquire about. "What about tonight? Where am I going to sleep with Lola?"

"I have a plan for that."

Jon shot Rocky a sideways glance from beneath one cocked brow. "Do you? Wanna fill me and her in on that?"

"Sure." Rocky nodded as he slowed the truck. "I made a call while we were at her apartment. They were booked full tonight but there was a vacancy for tomorrow night so I booked her a room on the base."

Jon nodded, a slow tipping of his head. "Good.

It's secure. Unexpected."

"Exactly." Rocky looked happy with the approval. "I'm hoping since Rick and his sister were willing to let me and Thom stay there tonight, the offer still stands now we found her."

Isabel watched the conversation happening over her, as if she weren't in the middle of both the situation and the two men talking.

Meanwhile, she couldn't help calculating how long she and Lola could survive on what little money she had saved while paying for a hotel room.

She'd have to work her shift tomorrow. She couldn't give up the tips she'd make working a prime shift anymore than she could leave the other girls shorthanded by not showing up.

But who would babysit while she did?

Having Hannah come to sit in her apartment had made her life so easy. And having Hannah's mother Dee right next door in case of an emergency had eased her worry.

Now, she had nobody.

Shit. She'd have to give up the shift.

As she obsessed, Rocky had pulled the truck along the curb and threw it into Park.

Jon's hand was already on the passenger door handle. "I'm gonna run in and talk to Rick quick. If he says yes about keeping her stuff here temporarily, I'll get him to move his truck so we can back up right to the garage door to unload."

"Sounds good. I'll wait here for your word." Rocky waited for Jon to slam the door before he turned to Isabel. "You're still worried."

Besides the fact she was ready to jump out of the

truck and run inside to see her daughter, Rocky was right. She was worried. About Tito. About work. About her life and her livelihood and her lack of a home and her future . . .

She glanced at him next to her and kept the growing list of concerns to herself. "How do you know?"

"That frown is one clue." He reached out and ran his thumb across her forehead over what she imagined must be creases deep enough he'd noticed them.

As his warm gentle touch sent emotions she couldn't identify through her, he dropped his hand back to the steering wheel and continued, "Besides that, I can see you're worried. From the way your fingers are turning white from lack of circulation because you've got your hands clutched so tight, to the way you're breathing. Quick and shallow. Like a scared bird."

It wasn't the most flattering description but he was right. She was terrified and she was terrible at hiding her feelings.

She felt the tears creeping behind her eyes, threatening to make themselves visible. "How am I ever going to face Tito and lie to him? I'm no good at lying. And I can't hide away at your friends' house or on your military base forever. I have to work. I have a shift tomorrow—"

"We'll figure it out."

"You keep saying that." As the tears burned her eye sockets she drew in a stuttering breath.

"And I mean it every time." Rocky lifted his chin in the direction of the house. "Rick's moving his truck for us. We'll unload then go on in and figure this Tito stuff all out."

"I still don't know how."

He turned his gaze on her. "You don't know who you're dealing with here."

"No, I guess not. Who am I dealing with?"

"The best of the best." He grinned and threw the truck into gear as she wondered who exactly she'd enlisted to help her.

CHAPTER EIGHT

"She looked scared to death during the drive over." Rocky's gaze cut to the closed bedroom door.

Isabel and Lola were in there, the results of a discussion with Darci about Isabel needing to feed Lola. That had put some pretty inappropriate images into his head. Now all he kept thinking about was Isabel's breasts.

"We probably scared the hell out of her." Jon glanced at Rick. "We entered the apartment like it was a close quarters battle training exercise."

Rocky snorted at the sad truth of what Jon said. "Yup. We sure did."

At least the conversation had dragged his attention off his inappropriate thoughts of Isabel inside that bedroom breastfeeding. He was obviously one sick motherfucker.

"Besides you guys showing off your advanced

combat skills in suburbia, she's got a lot to be concerned about." Rick spun his laptop so Rocky could see the screen. "Take a look. Here's what my contact in Miami sent me on her boyfriend."

"*Ex*-boyfriend." Rocky corrected.

Rick cocked up one brow. "Ex or not, he's bad news."

Rocky scanned the email, landing on the signature line. "You have a contact in the Miami police department?"

"Damn right, I do. Sierra's got a house down there. I made it a priority the minute I took over as her head of security."

A house in Miami. A suite at the Ritz here. Rick sure had stepped in it when he landed Academy Award winner Sierra Cox as a girlfriend.

If she was as high maintenance as Rocky assumed she was, Rick could keep her. Though Rick's Miami contact was proving useful . . . and concerning.

Everything in that email convinced Rocky they couldn't underestimate this Tito guy.

Jon's cell vibrated where it lay on the table. He glanced at the display. "It's Zane. He said he'd get back to us after he'd spoken to his contacts in D.C. about the immigration issue." Jon hit a button and said, "Hey, Zane. I've got you on speaker. Rocky and Rick are with me."

"Hey, sorry it took so long. I had to track the senator down on the golf course." Zane's voice came through the cell phone speaker. He sounded weary.

"And?" Rocky asked, afraid of the answer. "This

is Rocky, by the way."

"Hi, Rocky. So long story short, he basically told me that since the US opened relations with Cuba, the whole thing's one big cluster fuck. Your girl would have been better off before the change. Then she could have tried for political asylum. Apparently things being better between our countries makes it worse for her situation."

"So what, she's screwed? They're just going to send her back?" Rocky wasn't going to let that happen.

Tito had connections all over, according to his very long file from the Miami police. No doubt he could get to Isabel there, probably more easily than he could here.

"I didn't say that. We can file some papers. I can get them to the right people and hopefully push the process along a little faster, but it's still going to take time."

"Can you forward any information or documents we'll need to my email address?" Jon asked.

"Copy them to my email too. We can print them out here and get the ball rolling right away," Rick added.

"You got it, but I'm warning you it could take awhile. Even with my connections."

"How long is awhile?" Rocky asked, once again dreading Zane's response.

"Possibly months."

Rocky drew in a deep breath. "Okay. Thanks for your help, Zane."

"No problem. Talk to you guys later."

"Bye." Jon disconnected the call and glanced at

Rocky. "You don't look happy."

"I'm not." Rocky met his blue gaze. "Don't get me wrong. You guys are amazing. Rick's Miami contact and Zane's connections in the Capital. I don't know what Isabel would do without you."

He meant every word of it. Everyone had been incredible, taking on this problem as their own.

Currently Thom was outside patrolling the neighborhood on what was supposed to be his day off and the girls were out on the deck watching the food on the grill because Rick was inside on the computer.

"But?" Jon prompted.

"It seems like all we have are problems, when what we need are solutions. And something that won't take months to implement."

"I hear you. But we're working it. You've got a place for her for tonight. And for as long as you're stateside and they have a vacancy, she can stay at the lodge on base."

"That's half the problem. I can get sent on a mission at any time."

"I know that." Jon's measured reply had Rocky feeling bad he'd snapped at him.

"I know you do. I'm sorry. I'm just frustrated."

"I know that too." Jon nodded.

"The whole situation sucks. Hell, maybe you should just marry her. Circumvent everybody." Rick snorted out a laugh and stood. "I'm going to check the meat. I don't trust them out there alone with the grill."

As Rick went outside Rocky's brain spun trying to come up with some way to solve Isabel's problems with the ex and with her visa. No solutions presented themselves except for Rick's crazy suggestion.

Darci and Ali came back into the house, which left Rick and his girlfriend outside on the deck during what was an unseasonably warm and sunny afternoon. A day Rocky would have enjoyed far more if it weren't for the cloud of the threat hanging over Isabel and her daughter.

Before he could sink further into depression, the front door swung open and had him spinning toward it just as Chris Cassidy's bulk filled the doorway.

"We're here and we're hungry." Chris made a beeline for the kitchen and scooped Darci into a hug that lifted her off the floor. After a kiss that matched the enthusiasm of the embrace, Chris said, "I missed you, darlin'."

"I missed you too." Rick's sister looked absolutely smitten as she playfully hit Chris's wide chest with one fist. "Now put me down and I'll get you and Brody a bowl of chili."

"Put her down, bro. I'm starving." Brody closed the front door and moved into the room. "Six hours on the road and Chris wouldn't let us stop to eat even once."

"Sorry. I was anxious to get here. Besides, you're crazy if you wanna eat truck stop food when there's Darci's homemade chili waiting on us."

"Here you two go." Ali slid two bowls of steaming chili onto the island as Darci went to the drawer and got out cutlery. "And it's probably a good thing you came straight here without stopping. We had a little excitement."

Chris's brows rose as he glanced at Ali and then to the men in the dining room. "Oh did you?"

Brody lowered a loaded spoon without taking a bite. "What's going on? What'd we miss?"

"Well, let's see. First there was a baby left on the doorstep. And now there's a stripper in my bedroom." Darci laughed as she said it, but Rocky cringed at her words.

Maybe he shouldn't have asked if Isabel could stay the night.

Darci's announcement understandably elicited more questions from the Cassidy brothers who'd missed the day's worth of events. As Jon joined the discussion and started to explain what they'd done and what they knew so far, Rocky took the opportunity to go outside.

Rick glanced up from the grill as Rocky slid the glass door open. "Hey. These'll be done in a few."

Rocky tipped his head. "The Cassidy boys will be happy to hear that. They just got here."

"Did they?" Rick's girlfriend's eyes widened. "Good. I'm going to go inside."

"Yeah. Go ahead."

Once she was gone through the door Rocky frowned at Rick. "What was that about?"

Rick rolled his eyes. "She's reading for a movie about a woman from Alabama."

It took a second for all the pieces to fall together in Rocky's mind. "So she wants to hang around Chris and Brody because they're from there?"

"Yup. She says she needs to listen to how they talk."

Rocky laughed. "Okay . . . Anyway, I wanted to

make sure it was really okay that Isabel and Lola spend the night here. And me too."

"Of course. It's fine. I said it was."

"Yeah, but are you sure it's okay with Darci?"

"Sure. She can sleep at Chris's place. No big deal. She sleeps over there a couple of times a week anyway."

"I wasn't sure. Darci doesn't seem too happy."

Rick raised his gaze from where he'd been transferring the meat from the grill to a platter. A frown creased his brow. "Why do you say that?"

"She just made a comment about a stripper sleeping in her bed. It's no big deal to get a hotel room out in town. Really. I'll just stop by the base and grab the rest of my weapons. I can sit watch all night. I've done it before."

"Dude. No. It's fine."

"You sure? Darci—"

"Darci has a chip on her shoulder about the strip club. That's my own fault. I should have never told her how much we used to hang out there. Now she's dating Chris, she hates the idea he used to go there."

"Understood. So given that, are you sure it's okay?"

"Positive."

Rocky finally accepted the answer. "Okay. Thanks."

"No problem. Can you get the door?"

"Sure." Rocky slid the door open and moved out of the way to let Rick and the overloaded platter through.

As he slid the door closed behind them, he glanced in the direction of the bedroom.

The scent of the barbecued meat Rick had carried past was almost enough to distract him from the presence of the woman in Darci's bed.

Almost, but not quite.

CHAPTER NINE

The baby stirring woke Isabel. It took a few minutes to get her bearings and remember why she was in a strange room, sleeping on top of the covers in her clothes with the baby on the bed next to her.

It was dark. The only light in the room came from the illuminated face of the clock on the nightstand and a crack beneath the door where a thin strip of light slipped inside from the hallway.

It had still been light outside when she had closed her eyes, intent on just resting for a moment after feeding Lola. She'd obviously fallen asleep.

The house was quiet except for the distant sound of a television playing softly somewhere.

As Isabel got her brain working again, Lola made her desires known. The baby had started quietly cooing but after being made to wait for her meal, she wound up and let out a wail.

"Shh, I'm here. I'll feed you." She pulled herself

into a sitting position and while propped against the bed pillows, lifted the wiggling, squalling babe.

After three months, Isabel could—and had on occasion—fed her daughter while being half asleep herself. The practice helped her now as she opened her nursing bra and positioned the baby.

It wasn't more than a couple of minutes before a soft knock on the door startled her. Luckily, Lola was too involved in eating to be upset by her mother nearly jumping out of her skin.

Surprised by the knock at this time of night, Isabel didn't have much choice except to say, "Come in."

The door swung in slowly and she could see Rocky, silhouetted in the light in the hallway.

"Um, hey." He spoke in a loud whisper. She didn't know if that was for Lola's benefit, or to avoid waking whoever else was still in the house. "I heard the baby so I figured you were awake."

"Yeah. She was hungry. Sorry if her crying woke you."

"No. I was up. Um, you fell asleep without eating dinner. There's a ton of leftovers and Rick and Darci told me to help myself so if you wanted something, I could, you know, heat it up for you. When you're done with . . . uh . . . what you're doing, of course."

Isabel smiled at how this man who always seemed in total control since she'd met him, couldn't seem to get out a simple sentence.

The sight of a woman breastfeeding was enough to have him stuttering and looking at the carpet rather than at her and the baby, even though they had to be barely visible in the shadows of the room.

"I am a little hungry. Thanks."

"Oh. Okay. Good. I'm glad I asked. I'll, uh, go get it heating for you. Um, what did you want? There's chili. And some hot dogs. And potato salad. A little of everything?"

She was kind of enjoying his discomfort. It made her feel like she was on even footing with him. It showed he was human. That he wasn't completely invincible and perfectly in control as he'd first appeared.

"Yeah. Sure. Thanks."

"Okay. I'm gonna go get you a plate."

She nodded. "Okay. Thank you."

He waved away her thanks. "No problem. Happy to, you know, help. So, um, yeah. I'll be back."

"Okay." Smiling, she watched him back out of the doorway like there was a deadly tiger inside, rather than one woman breastfeeding a baby.

Lola had finished eating and was drifting off to sleep by the time Rocky's soft knock came once again on the bedroom door.

Luckily, he pushed the door open an inch and peeked inside so she didn't have to answer and disturb Lola.

She motioned him inside as she struggled to stand up without waking the baby. She needed to put Lola in her car seat. They'd both get better rest if the baby wasn't in the bed next to her. She eased the baby into the seat and snapped the straps to secure her.

When that was done, she glanced up at Rocky. He stood awkwardly nearby, plate and fork in hand.

"Thanks for the food," she whispered.

"No problem." He glanced at the sleeping infant. "Can you come out to the other room to eat?"

"Sure." She followed him as he turned and led the way to the living room.

It felt less like the middle of the night with the table lamp lit and a talk show playing on the television. Rocky put her meal down on the coffee table and motioned to the sofa.

"Sit and eat." It wasn't phrased as a request. More of a command.

She found herself doing as he asked. He was right. She couldn't remember the last meal she'd eaten and now that the food was in front of her and smelled so incredible she was hungry.

The realization had been easy to ignore during the stress of the past day but faced with a mouthful of chili that tasted like heaven she could no longer ignore her empty stomach, which made itself known with a loud grumble.

She pressed her hand to her belly and cringed as she glanced at Rocky.

"Told you. You needed to eat." He smiled.

The stress eased away a bit with every bite of food she swallowed, all while Rocky watched the show on the screen and gave her the time she needed to slowly unwind her tightly coiled nerves.

She should be used to stress by now. It had been her constant companion since the day she took that pregnancy test, but things had escalated quickly with the sudden reappearance of Tito.

The thought of him had her stomach clenching, but she took another forkful anyway. Even if she didn't eat for herself, she had to eat for Lola. She couldn't risk her milk drying up. It was too convenient to have the constant source of food for the baby in case they ended up on the run.

God she hoped it didn't come to that. But she didn't know how to make this town safe for them again now that Tito had found her.

There were still a few bites left on the plate when she set it down on the table.

Rocky glanced at the dish and then to her. "You wanna talk?"

Want to? No. But she supposed she needed to. "I'm supposed to work at the club tomorrow. My usual babysitter is my neighbor's daughter but now I'm afraid to leave Lola with her."

He turned to face her better. "Call in sick."

"I need the money."

"I'll loan you money." Again, his tone made it seem more like an order than an offer. This was a man who seemed used to making a decision and then seeing it through to completion.

She sighed. "That's very generous of you, but taking time off from work and you giving me a loan is not a long term solution. What are we going to do about Tito?"

"Any chance he'll give up and go away?"

Isabel let out a short bitter laugh. "Not likely. I hurt his pride leaving the way I did. He's not going to walk away without getting back at me. Saving face."

"Well maybe he'll have to." Rocky pointedly avoiding eye contact and focusing solely on the television had Isabel frowning.

"What are you saying?"

"Nothing. Just, you know, if he's as bad as you say, there's a good chance he could be on the run from the law at any minute. Then he wouldn't have time to come after you. He'll have more important things to worry about."

Her eyes widened. "What did you do?"

"Me? I didn't do anything." Rocky's expression was so innocent she almost believed him.

He turned his focus back to the television. "I'll come with you to work tomorrow and sit in the back of the club. Make sure there's no trouble. Ali and Darci will watch the baby."

"You can't offer that without asking them first."

"Ali already offered to babysit if you needed her. I think she's got a little baby lust. Jon's not happy about it. Between you and me I think he's a bit of a commitment-phobe, but it'll be fine. No worries." Rocky shot her a grin and then stood. "You done with this?"

"Yes."

"Want dessert? There's some berry cobbler left. Ali made it. It was real good."

Cobbler. It sounded so normal, so comforting, so indicative of everything her life had been missing lately that she nodded. "Okay. Thanks."

"No problem." Genuine warmth shone through his smile.

There were genuinely nice guys in the world. Rocky was proof. It was a damn shame she hadn't found a guy like him a year ago.

Too late. Tito's existence in her and Lola's life was a reality, ruining the chance of her getting a degree, or a good job, or a nice guy like Rocky—for at least the foreseeable future.

Rocky came back into the room just as the tears overcame her. He stopped dead in his tracks and looked at her with concern, the steaming dessert on a plate in his hand.

Isabel swiped away the tears. "Sorry."

Shaking his head, he put the dish on the table and sat next to her. "Don't apologize."

"You've just been so nice and—" She couldn't get any more words out as she started shaking.

Her chest heaved as breathing got more difficult the harder she cried.

He wrapped one arm around her shoulders and pulled her against him. She felt the support of his warmth and strength.

Rocky mumbled a string of colorful obscenities that had something to do with Tito. His creative swearing on her behalf, combined with how much safer she felt from even this small amount of contact, elicited a laugh she didn't know she was capable of.

Drawing in a deep calming breath, she wiped away the last of the tears. "Thank you."

"For what?" he asked.

"For making me laugh. For the food. For the bed. And the use of the truck . . ." The list was too long to name all he'd already done for her.

"That?" He let out a snort. "That was all nothing."

She heard the subtext of the meaning behind his words without his having to say it.

The hard part was still ahead of them.

She glanced down at the plate Rocky had brought her containing the cobbler Ali had made, sitting on the table in Rick and Darci's house and she realized that for the first time in months of being on the run, her biggest regret was not being able to settle down long enough to have friends like these wonderful people.

CHAPTER TEN

He'd been at the club for fun countless times, which made it particularly odd being there today for this self appointed close personal protection assignment.

Enlightening was an even better word than odd.

Rocky usually thought of himself as more observant than the average person. It came with the job. But it was becoming more than obvious that he sure as hell didn't employ his skills of observation when he came to the club looking for mindless pleasure.

How many hours had he sat in this very room and never noticed the security cameras? And was the music always so god-awful and so loud?

His phone vibrated in the pocket of the jacket he wore to hide his shoulder holster. He pulled it out and saw Rick's name on the readout.

He hit the button to answer and pressed it to his

ear. “Hey.”

“Where are you?” Rick asked, though it was damn hard to hear him.

“I’m still at the club. Her shift’s got another two hours or so.”

“Any sign of Isabel’s Latin lover yet?”

Rocky hated that reference. It reminded him too much that a man who didn’t come close to deserving Isabel in any way had already had all of the pleasures with her that Rocky could only dream of experiencing.

“Nope. Just a handful of young sailors with their attention glued to the girls.”

And the three minutes that Isabel had been on stage in front of the leering boys had been pretty damn stressful . . . for both of them.

She’d kept her eyes on the audience, no doubt watching for Tito. Rocky had done the same, while keeping just as close an eye on the kids from the base to make sure none of them got out of line with her.

Then there was the other thing that he had to deal with—trying not to leer himself.

He couldn’t believe he’d never noticed Isabel before, because she was exactly his type. A dark-haired beauty rounded in all the right places.

Of course, he’d been away a lot and she had to be new here given the fact she’d had Lola only a few months ago.

“Tough job you assigned yourself there, bud.” Rick’s displeasure at the division of labor came through clearly in his tone and brought Rocky back to the conversation.

Even if he hadn't heard the baby crying in the background above the sound of the music in the club, Rocky would have known Rick was unhappy.

"What's up with Lola?" he asked.

"No clue. Darci and Ali changed her. Fed her. Danced around with her while singing songs. We're running out of ideas here."

"Not that I know what I'm doing any more than you do, but did you burp her?"

"I'll pass that question on to the girls and see if they did."

"I can grab Isabel and ask her if you really need—"

"Nah. Don't bother her yet. She's got enough to worry about. If we can't get the baby settled down soon, I'll give you a call back. Maybe I'll call Thom."

Rocky laughed at that. "I think you should. Why shouldn't he get to share in the fun?"

"Right. Oh, and Jon just left. He said he's going to keep an eye on the club parking lot. Make sure Tito's not hoping to get to her there."

"Good idea."

Rick snorted. "My opinion? He just wanted to get away from the babysitting duty but yeah, it was a sound enough plan I couldn't stop him from going. And there's no way Darci will let me or Chris leave when she and Ali are stuck here with the kid."

"Chris is there too?"

"Yup. One of the duties of dating my sister. He has to do what she says. But he's as useless when it comes to babies as the rest of us." Rick paused. "Oh thank God, she's quiet."

"What did you do?"

The sound of Rick walking was followed by a soft laugh. "It looks like Chris got the idea to put her on top of the dryer while it's running."

"Jesus. Is that safe?"

"She's strapped in the car seat. We'll have to watch and make sure the seat doesn't vibrate off but hell, that's worth it for some quiet."

Rocky cringed at the image of Lola and the seat toppling off the machine. "Please don't let her fall on her head."

"Dude, I think four adults can handle one tiny baby."

Rick hadn't sounded so certain of that just a few minutes ago, but Rocky let it go. "I'll call to check in later."

"You just worry about Sanchez. We got it covered."

"I'm calling anyway."

"Fine. Talk to you later." Rick disconnected and Rocky tried to not worry.

"Another water?"

Rocky turned to the bartender and saw the unhappy expression on his face. He reached for his wallet and pulled out a bill. "You can make it a diet soda this time. I'm sorry. I'm not drinking today."

The hulking older man reached for a glass as he eyed Rocky. "You're not watching the girls all that much either, so what are you doing here?"

"Just helping out a friend."

The man glanced around the bar. "Well, you were here before them." He lifted a chin in the direction of the seamen, all clad in NAVY T-shirts. "And they don't look like they need any help from you, so I'm figuring it must be one of my girls."

"*Your* girls?"

He tipped his head. "Yup. I'm the owner of this club."

"Oh." He turned to face the man more fully and extended his right hand. "Rocky Mangiano."

The man gripped his with his own beefy hand. "Pete O'Neill. You Navy?"

No use denying that. It was on the damn bumper sticker on his truck in the parking lot. He should probably peel that thing off but for now, he nodded. "Yeah."

"You involved with one of my dancers?"

"No. Well, yes, but not in the way you're insinuating."

"Wasn't insinuating anything. I'm outright asking." The man's gaze was steady as it held Rocky's.

Rocky was usually a pretty good judge of character and this man struck him as trustworthy. "Isabel."

The man's brows rose. "Since you know the name I cut her checks to and not her stage name, I'm going to take that as a yes, you are involved."

"It's not as simple as that." Rocky leaned in, keeping is voice as low as he could and still be heard over the pounding dance music. "You know she has a kid?"

"I think I've heard that, yeah."

"Well, I'm here to make sure both Isabel and Lola stay safe."

"Safe from whom?"

"Someone from her past who's bad news."

"The kid's father?"

Surprised he'd guessed, Rocky said, "I didn't say that."

"You didn't have to." The bartender leaned closer. "I figured there was some reason she showed up here looking for a job. We get all kinds of girls working here, but not usually like her."

"Meaning what? What's she like?"

"Shy. Timid almost." He shook his head. "Her audition was so bad, I honestly only gave her the job because I felt sorry for her."

Rocky frowned. "She didn't look so bad up there today."

"That's because the other girls took her under their wing. Taught her. She's a quick learner and a hard worker. Now she's got a couple of months here, you'd never know she was so completely wrong for this job when she started."

Rocky wasn't sure if Isabel being such an accomplished stripper now was a good thing, but he could agree completely she was bright and a hard worker. He could see that himself.

"You know, I pride myself on making sure my girls are safe."

"I didn't mean any offense that you're not doing a good job, but we're not talking an overzealous admirer here."

"I guess not or she wouldn't need hired muscle."

Rocky snorted. "Since she's not paying me, I'm not exactly hired muscle."

"No. You're just a friend."

Rocky nodded. "Yup."

The bartender pulled his mouth into a crooked smile. "Okay. Got it. And if she needs any time off to deal with this situation, she's got it. The girls are good about taking extra shifts."

"Thanks. That's helpful. I'll tell her. She was worried about taking time off."

"No problem. Oh, and by the way, your *friend* is about to take the stage again."

Rocky spun toward the raised, spotlighted wooden runway as the bartender chuckled behind him.

At the moment, he didn't give a shit what the club's owner thought. Besides, the man was right. Rocky wanted to be much more than Isabel's friend . . . particularly now as she strutted her stuff across the stage.

He'd never felt so torn in all his life. Half of him wanted to wrap a blanket around her to hide the costume that showed much too much skin. He'd love to jump up on that stage, toss her over his shoulder and take her far away from all the gawking eyes on her now.

The other half of him had gone dry in the mouth as he watched her bend at the waist and stick her tempting ass high in the air. That half wanted to jump on stage too, but not to cover her up. Rather to strip her down and take what she so artfully offered.

It was just a show, he reminded himself. That offer wasn't real at all and it wasn't for him. It was for every man in the room willing to part with a dollar—or twenty—so she could pay her rent and support her daughter.

That thought brought him back around full circle and he wanted her off that stage and back safe at Rick's place with Lola.

He noticed the icy glass of soda the bartender had set on the cocktail napkin by his elbow on the bar. Rocky drew in a long slow sip through the straw.

Maybe he should order a drink. Between the guilt, the desire, and the hard-on pressing against the zipper of his jeans he sure as hell felt like he needed one about now.

The guilt wasn't enough to keep his eyes off the stage though, or his mind from slipping into lurid thoughts of Isabel.

He should probably just go sit with that group of drooling sailors who were now standing so they could better shove dollar bills into the very few items she still had on.

Rocky curled his hand into a fist and drew in an angry breath.

The bartender's laugh had him glancing at the man, who grinned and shook his head. "It takes a lot of strength to be able to handle falling for a girl in this profession."

He opened his mouth to say he hadn't fallen for her, until he realized he didn't believe his own bullshit, so there was no way the bartender was going to.

Instead, Rocky tipped his head. "Yeah. I'm starting to realize that."

CHAPTER ELEVEN

To say her shift at the club had been strange would be a vast understatement.

Young guys from one of the local Navy bases were the usual clientele for a weekend afternoon, but having Rocky watching her for all the hours during which she worked made everything seem different.

Isabel hadn't been that self-conscious since her first week of working at the club. Yes, that was only a couple of months ago but it seemed a lifetime.

It might as well have been.

She usually tuned out the audience as much as possible when on stage. The glare of the lights made it easy enough to do.

Those same lights made it almost impossible for her to actually see Rocky seated in the back of the room at the bar, but he was there. She felt him. Felt his gaze on her.

Felt—or at least imagined—what he thought of

the job she'd had to resort to as he watched her on stage. Letting men shove bills into her G-string. Taking her clothes off for money.

Isabel opened the door of her locker and shoved the bills she held in her fist into the inside pocket in her oversized tote bag. After safely zipping away the tips that would help to pay for a hotel room until she could go back to her apartment, if she ever could, she fished in the bottom of the bag for her cell phone.

One glance at the multiple notifications on the readout had her heart pounding. Scrolling down she saw a missed call, a text and a voicemail, all from her neighbor.

It could be nothing. Maybe Hannah was just wondering if Isabel needed a babysitter this week.

Or it could be something—like Tito snooping around the apartment again.

The only way to find out would be to call—and that scared the hell out of her because in some misguided effort at self-preservation not knowing felt safer than knowing.

She was wrong of course, but she hadn't been right a whole lot lately so . . .

Meanwhile, her battery icon was showing in the red. She could only hope her battery lasted long enough so she could listen to and deal with whatever the message from her neighbor was.

She needed to plug in her phone. To do that she had to find where she'd put her charger yesterday during the great exodus from the apartment. It had to be with her stuff stashed at Rick and Darci's house. Either in her suitcase in Darci's bedroom or in the garage in one of the many bags of stuff.

She let out a long shaky breath.

"Everything okay?"

Isabel spun away from her locker to see Jasmine had come into the dressing room. "Yeah. Fine. I just missed a call and my battery's dead so I can't get the voicemail."

"You worried that call is about the ex?" Leaning in to check her makeup, Jasmine met Isabel's gaze in the reflection of the mirror as she asked the question.

The other dancers were all aware she had a baby and that the situation with her ex was bad, which is why she'd left Miami. When she'd arrived today she'd revealed the latest to Jasmine.

She'd realized early on that she needed to tell them about the situation. The girls could be in danger because of her. Tito had never cared much about collateral damage.

"I'm a little worried that call from my neighbor might be to tell me he was back snooping around my apartment. Not that there's anything there for him to find anymore since I moved out."

There wasn't much that survived Rocky and Jon's sweep. Some food in the cabinets and fridge was allowed to stay but only if it didn't hint at Lola's existence. Everything else went.

Jasmine turned to face her. "Anything you need, you know you've got it. Money. A sofa to crash on."

The generous offer from her coworker, on top of the stress that already had worn her down, had Isabel tearing up. She drew in a breath to settle herself. "So far I've got it covered. But thank you."

"Where are you staying? A hotel?"

"Actually, this is going to sound strange, but you know Rocky? The Navy guy who's here sometimes. The one with the beard."

Jasmine's eyes widened. "If you mean the one who was here for your entire shift today, then yeah, I know him."

"I stayed with him at his friends' house last night." Isabel decided she'd better expand her explanation as Jasmine looked as if she was making assumptions. Untrue assumptions. "His friend's sister stayed at her boyfriend's place and let me and Lola sleep in her room and Rocky slept on the sofa in the living room. Though actually I'm not sure he slept at all. I think he stayed up all night keeping watch for Tito."

All her babbling did was reinforce the shock visible on Jasmine's face.

"I didn't know you knew him. I've never seen you even talk to him." Jasmine folded her arms and waited.

"I didn't." She sighed. "It's a long story. I'm sorry. He's still yours when he's here. You know, for any lap dances or . . . whatever. I wouldn't steal your customer."

Isabel swallowed hard as it hit her. Her knight in shining armor might have saved her, but he also knew Jasmine, possibly intimately.

She liked Rocky. A lot. Liked him as much as she hated the image of him being with Jasmine and probably the other girls too.

Various scenarios involving Rocky and her

fellow dancers ran in her head. It was enough to have her stomach churning.

Jasmine snorted out a laugh. "It's okay. He's not mine. I don't know what you did, but he's clearly yours now. It's pretty obvious he's only got eyes for you."

Isabel shook her head. "I didn't do—"

Jasmine held up one hand and interrupted Isabel's defense of herself. "This happens all the time. I can dance a hundred times for a guy in the back room, but inevitably he'll meet a girl who he's interested in for more than just dances."

"He's just helping me because of Tito."

It wasn't because he only had eyes for her, as Jasmine had said. That was crazy. Ridiculous.

Even with as nice as the idea would be that a man like Rocky would be interested in her in spite of the mess she'd made of her life, it would never happen.

"Sweetie, I know men. It's more than just helping you he's after."

Again, Isabel shook her head. "I don't think so." Her friend Jasmine said she knew men, but she was wrong about Rocky, even if she did know him well. Isabel swallowed the bitter taste in her throat at that thought. "Jas. Did you and Rocky . . . Um, have you and he—"

"Have I done the deed with your man? No, sweetie. Never."

The question that had been poking at her had come out before Isabel could stop it, but now that she had asked it, she wasn't sure she believed the answer.

"But you know he has a tattoo . . . down there."

Jasmine smiled. "One of the girls who used to work here part time also worked at the tattoo studio. She did his tattoo."

"Oh." The relief flooded her.

"Now that that's settled, you might want to get moving. Your man is waiting outside for you to finish up in here. I saw him hanging around eyeballing the hallway when I came back."

"He's not my man." Isabel rolled her eyes, but still couldn't squelch how giddy hearing Rocky called that made her. She pulled her bag out and slammed the locker door. "But I guess I should go."

"Dressed like that?"

She was almost to the door when Jasmine's comment stopped her. She turned in time to see Jasmine's gaze drop down her body as she smirked.

Isabel smothered a curse that would have gotten her a hundred Hail Marys from her grandmother as punishment back when she was younger in Cuba.

She glanced down at her costume, or what remained of it after her dance. "I have to change."

Jasmine lifted a brow. "You sure? I think your new beau might enjoy that outfit."

Screwing up her mouth, Isabel shot her so-called friend a glare and opened her bag. She pulled out yoga pants, a T-shirt and ballet flats. She'd throw on her clothes and then she'd find Rocky and they could both go to Rick and Darci's so she could safely collect Lola. Because that was what this was all about. Keeping Lola safe. Nothing more.

But it would sure be nice if it were.

CHAPTER TWELVE

Rocky had taken to pacing by the time he glanced up and finally saw Isabel emerge from the dancers' hallway. He'd been about two minutes from heading back there and looking for her.

It had been a stupid move on his part to not have checked out the back himself the moment they'd arrived. Made sure Tito couldn't get in through some back door to grab her.

If he'd been so lax on a mission, it could easily cost lives. They might not be in a warzone or some hostile region, but Tito was no less of a threat when it came to Isabel's safety.

Next time he'd be more careful . . . if there was a next time. As it was, it was looking less and less likely that he'd be able to sit watch during another one of her shifts.

He pocketed that thought and forced a smile as Isabel neared. "Hey. You ready to go?"

"Yes. Sorry I took so long. I had to change my clothes. We can go."

"Not a problem. Um, so—" He didn't get the rest of the words he needed to out as she interrupted him.

"When we get to the house I really need to find my cell charger." Not realizing he had something to say, she continued talking as they pushed through the exit and into the waning light of early evening. "My phone just powered off because the battery is dead but before it did I saw there was a message from my neighbor."

That information gave him pause as he opened the passenger door of his truck. "The same neighbor who told you that Tito had been looking for you at your apartment?"

"Yes."

Before she climbed into the cab of his pickup he could see the worry beneath the glitter still dusting her face. Funny how the presence of the glitter he usually despised didn't bother him on her.

He shoved that notion aside and considered the unheard voicemail from her neighbor. He understood her concern completely. He'd like to know what that message said himself. The sooner the better.

Forewarned was forearmed.

He walked around and climbed into the driver's seat. "What kind of phone do you have?"

She held up her cell. He saw that his charger wouldn't work on her phone.

One more piece of bad luck added on to the shit pile of his day.

“Okay. We’ll find your charger when we get to Rick’s.”

That put an end to Rocky’s plans to tell her his bad news, at least until they found out what the message from her neighbor was about. Rocky’s worse fear had come true. Command hadn’t confirmed it yet but all the signs were there—he was about to be called in.

The text had arrived about an hour ago. He had to be at the base at the crack of dawn.

He’d stepped outside of the club and taken his eyes off Isabel only long enough to call his commander, Grant Milton.

Rocky had asked about the possibility of putting in a request for time off. After Grant had asked if it was a matter of life or death, and Rocky had to tell the truth and say no, the request was swiftly squashed.

If he had to wager a guess, he’d say there was a good chance they’d be shipping right out after the meeting tomorrow.

He should have realized this was coming. There was always shit happening around the globe, but incidents had increased lately, becoming closer together, more deadly.

With the recent ramped up Coalition offense against ISIS the retaliations had been coming steadily. Bombs in a café in Turkey and a park in Pakistan. The deadly attacks on the US firebase in northern Iraq. The Brussels airport and metro bombings.

It was only a matter of time before command would call his team in. This meeting and Grant’s rejection of his request was a sign that time had come.

The only question left was where they'd be sent and for how long.

He couldn't get the time off he needed to deal with the Tito situation. He likely wouldn't even be in the country. So what was he supposed to do to protect her?

She was safe while she was physically on the base, but how long would they let her stay in the room he'd booked without him being there? He didn't want her at a hotel out in town. Hell, he didn't even want her going to work but he knew she wouldn't give that up and accept a loan easily. She was too proud.

The more he thought about it the more he was certain, he couldn't leave Isabel on her own, unprotected. But neither could he dump the responsibility on Jon or the guys from GAPS. The GAPS team had assignments of their own that took them far and wide on a moment's notice too.

By the time Rocky had pulled the truck into Rick's neighborhood, he was ill about the whole thing.

He'd take on any mission anywhere fearlessly but this situation—having his hands tied and being unable to help Isabel when she needed it—knocked the wind right out of him and had him feeling completely helpless.

At the sight of the house, Rick's words from the day before flew into Rocky's brain.

Marry her.

It was a crazy idea . . . and the more he thought

about it, the better he liked it.

Rick might have been joking at the time, but what he suggested was actually a damn good plan. Possibly the only plan at the moment.

Heart beating faster as the idea flew through his mind Rocky parked and cut the engine. Shaking, he got out and ran around the truck to open Isabel's door.

Independent woman that she was, she already had the door open. He waited for her to step down and slammed the door behind her.

At the front door of the house, Thom answered their knock. "Hey, come on in. Boy, are we happy to see you."

Uh, oh.

"Why?" Rocky asked.

"Nothing bad, but I think Lola's about to start teething. She's, uh, cranky."

Isabel was in the house and heading toward the sound of Lola's wails before Rocky made it through the front door.

"Everything else okay?" he asked.

"Yeah. No sign of anyone. I've done a few sweeps of the neighborhood. Jon got back about half an hour ago so he's been keeping an eye out too."

Rocky glanced around the house. "Where's Rick?"

"He conveniently had some official event with Sierra tonight so he abandoned us about an hour ago."

Rocky glanced into the kitchen to see Chris, Darci, Ali and Jon all huddled around the high chair where an unhappy Lola was being lifted by Isabel.

He laughed. "Dude, you still had five adults to take care of one baby. Rick didn't exactly abandon you."

"You listen to that crying for a few hours and get back to me." Thom glanced at the kitchen and leaned in. "Don't tell your girl but we even resorted to rubbing scotch on Lola's gums."

"Jesus. You can go to jail for doing shit like that."

Thom scowled. "It was a few drops on my finger. That's all. We didn't give her a bottle full to drink. And my mother did the same to me when I was teething. Yours probably did too, so get off your high horse and babysit yourself next time."

"The next time might not be for a while. You got the text about the meeting, right?"

"Yeah. You thinking we're getting sent out?" Thom asked, voice still low.

They were the only two in the house still on active duty.

Chris and Jon might be former SEALs but officially they were civilians now, as were the three women. There was a good chance they'd guess, but they couldn't be privy to the details of the team's movements or missions.

"I'm almost positive. I called Grant and asked about the chances of getting some time off to deal with this shit and the answer was a firm no."

"I think Brody agrees with you. He texted me saying he couldn't come over because he wanted to get on Skype with his girl in Alabama in case we end up leaving tomorrow." Thom sighed. "Shit.

There goes my plan to drive home next weekend."

As much as it sucked that Thom couldn't go home to Massachusetts or Connecticut or wherever to visit his parents and his girlfriend for the weekend, Rocky had more pressing issues.

He decided to get Thom's take on the situation since he was the only one there who'd ever been married or had kids.

While everyone else was occupied in the kitchen, Rocky tipped his head toward the back door. "Come outside with me for a second."

Thom didn't question the request. He just nodded and said, "Okay."

After they'd walked across the room and out the sliding door to the deck, Rocky glanced sideways at Thom. "Rick said something yesterday."

Thom let out a laugh. "Rick usually has a lot to say about a whole lotta of things."

"Yeah, but this was particularly interesting."

"That's new. You going to share this mysterious wisdom from Rick or keep it to yourself?" Looking like a smartass with one brow cocked high, Thom leaned back against the railing, arms folded.

Rocky raised his eyes to meet Thom's gaze head-on. "He said I should marry Isabel."

Thom lifted his brows higher. "It was my understanding that baby in there isn't yours. Was I wrong?"

"No. She's not mine."

Frown firmly in place, Thom continued, "And I thought you barely knew Isabel."

"Correct. We met a couple of nights ago at the club." They may have only just met, but that didn't mean he didn't know her. He felt like they'd been through a lot together in a very short time. "But what if I did marry her?"

Thom's eyes widened. "Why? Rick was obviously joking when he suggested that. You can't take what he said seriously."

"I know he was, but if I did marry her then she couldn't get deported, and she and Lola could stay on base in family housing even while I'm deployed."

"But marriage is a legally binding contract." Thom's eyes couldn't have gotten any wider. "Believe me. I know from personal experience."

"I know it sounds crazy." Rocky held Thom's gaze. "But what do you think?"

"I completely agree with you. It's crazy." Thom drew in a breath and let it out slowly. "But if you're seriously considering this, I can't tell you what to do. It's your decision to make. It's your life."

That wasn't exactly an opinion Thom had rendered but Rocky supposed it didn't matter all that much what his friend and teammate thought about the idea. Thom was right. It was Rocky's life and his decision to make.

Well, his and Isabel's, which left one big question—what would she think about his proposal?

Proposal. Rocky swallowed away the dryness. It wasn't exactly how or why he'd ever imagined he'd propose or get married but hell, life was unpredictable.

Unlike Thom, Rocky might be lacking in marital expertise but when it came to knowing that life could and would throw you a curveball when you least expected it—that he knew well from personal experience.

Rocky let out a breath. "Okay. Moving on . . . we gotta find her cell charger or at least have her call her neighbor from another phone. There was a message she couldn't retrieve and I'm worried it's news about her dick ex."

"Damn. Okay. Let's go figure this shit out." Thom pushed off the railing and headed for the door to the house. As he reached for the handle he glanced over his shoulder at Rocky. "Wouldn't be so bad being married to her, I suppose. She could dance for you at home."

"Shut up." Rocky scowled at Thom and tried not to remember how he'd already thought the same thing himself.

CHAPTER THIRTEEN

Waiting for the phone to power on after she plugged it in was about as nerve wracking as waiting for the pregnancy test to turn pink all those months ago.

It wasn't lost on Isabel that both events that had caused her an agonizing amount of stress had everything to do with Tito—her biggest mistake. To date anyway.

She held her breath as the screen finally lit. The message took its time to load. By the time it did she was shaking as she hit to retrieve the voicemail.

Rocky was right next to her, concern on his face. His friends sat a bit farther away, across the room at the dining room table where Darci had set out leftovers from the day before. Their eyes were on her as she held the cell phone in her hand, rather than on the plates of food.

Isabel hit speakerphone so everyone would be

able to hear. She didn't have any secrets from these people at this point. They knew as much—or more about her than her few remaining friends and distant relatives.

Her neighbor's voice came through the speaker.

"*Hey, Izzy. Call me when you get this? Thanks.*"

The lack of details did nothing to alleviate her worry. Rather it ramped it up another notch.

"Call her." Rocky's voice was low and steady, firm and intense but showing none of the strain she felt.

Apparently he was incredibly calm in stressful situations or he was a much better actor than she was.

She could barely breathe as she attempted to make the call, first hitting the wrong button and almost sending a text message rather than redialing to return the call.

Finally she managed to select the correct sequence of buttons to connect to her neighbor.

She listened to the ringing as the sound of blood pumping fast through her veins rushed loud through her ears.

"Hello?" Her neighbor's voice came through the speaker of the cellphone, live this time.

"Hi, Dee. It's Isabel."

"Hi. Thanks for getting back to me."

"Sorry I missed your call. I was working and then my cell was dead—" She was babbling again. She forced herself to take a breath and cut to the real question. "Is everything all right there at the apartment?"

"Yes . . . and no. It's probably nothing but there

was a man knocking on your door. Pretty enthusiastically. When you didn't answer he came and knocked on my door."

Isabel felt sick to her stomach. Tito had a temper and she'd personally seen him misdirect it at innocent people.

"Did you talk to him?" She feared the answer.

"No. I pretended I wasn't home either, but I thought you should know."

"Good. Don't answer if he comes back."

"Izzy, are you okay? Who is this man?"

Isabel glanced up at Rocky. He nodded in answer to her unspoken question.

"He's Lola's father. I left him and Miami when I found out I was pregnant with her. He doesn't know."

"And you don't want him to know. I get it. Your secret's safe with me."

"Thank you."

"It's no problem. You think maybe he'll give up and go away?"

"Hopefully." Isabel said it but she sure didn't believe it. Not even a little. It wasn't in Tito's nature to give up. "Thanks again for telling me. I'm, uh, staying with friends for a few days so I won't be home, but I'll keep in touch."

"Please do. Hannah misses Lola."

That statement twisted Isabel's heart. Glassy eyed, she said, "Tell her Lola misses her too. Bye."

"Bye."

Isabel hit the button to disconnect the call. She raised her gaze to meet Rocky's. "He's not going to give up and go away."

He dipped his head. "I know. I didn't assume he would."

"So what do we do?" she whispered, unable to draw enough breath to speak any louder.

Now that Lola was settled, fed and down for a nap, Isabel had let her guard down. The pressures settled in around her. She felt it like a physical weight, pressing on her chest, dragging her down toward the floor.

"First of all, you're not going back to that apartment. As soon as you eat something—"

"I'm not hungry."

"Eat anyway." Rocky widened his eyes in warning and she realized she wasn't going to get away with not eating. He continued, "As soon as I see you eat something, we'll gather whatever you need for tonight and tomorrow and then check into the room on base."

"Okay." Hiding out on the base was a temporary solution but she'd take it for now.

"Come on. Sit down. We have things to talk about."

She sat in the empty chair Rocky guided her to and immediately had a full plate of food in front of her—courtesy of Darci.

"I have an idea about how to maybe get him off your track, for a little bit anyway. If nothing else, it will at least keep him away from your neighbor and her daughter," Jon said.

Isabel raised her gaze to Jon. "I'd like that."

Hannah and Dee didn't deserve trouble on her account.

"I'm going to stay at your apartment for a

while."

Across the table, Ali's eyes popped wide at Jon's offer. "You are?"

Apparently Jon's announcement was as much as a surprise to his girlfriend Ali as it was to Isabel.

Jon dipped his head. "It won't be long. Just for a few days. Only until Tito shows up and I can tell him Isabel moved out and I'm moving in."

Rocky nodded. "It's a good idea. That would throw him off the track. Maybe he'll leave town thinking that Izzy moved on."

"Izzy?" Isabel cocked a brow at Rocky's use of the shortened version of her name.

He smiled. "That's what your neighbor called you. I like it. Do you mind?"

"No." In the midst of all the hell and upheaval, Rocky calling her Izzy was a small thing, yet it seemed oddly comforting.

"Good." He reached out and laid his hand over hers. "There's something else I think we should consider doing to keep you safe."

Rocky glanced up at the people around the table.

With Chris still out on patrol, the group gathered silently around the table watching her conversation with Rocky consisted of Darci, Ali, Jon and Thom.

It was Thom who stood up. "I think maybe we should give them some privacy for a few minutes."

Darci's eyes flew wide. "Why? What do you know that I don't?" She glanced to Ali and Jon. "Do you two know anything?"

Ali let out a snort. "I think it's pretty obvious I'm the last to know quite a few things."

Jon sighed at that verbal slam but didn't respond.

"Thanks, Thom. I'd appreciate a few minutes alone with her."

Isabel whipped her head around to stare at Rocky. "What's going on?"

"I'm going to tell you." Rocky smiled.

Darci let out a humph. "Just not us."

"I don't care if Thom fills you in on everything. I'd just like to not overwhelm Izzy anymore than necessary by making this a group discussion. Please?" Rocky appealed directly to Darci, probably since she looked the most unhappy about being asked to leave.

In her defense, this was her house. And Isabel and Lola were already an uninvited inconvenience that had displaced her from her bed last night, and her dining room now.

"Rocky, I don't mind if they stay." Isabel made an effort to appease her hostess.

Thom was already standing by the back door, poised to lead the way to the deck when Darci said, "No, it's okay. We can give you two privacy."

"Thank you." Rocky nodded. As the three followed Thom out, Rocky turned to fully face Isabel.

"Rocky, you're scaring me."

He squeezed the hand he still held in his. "It's nothing to be scared about."

"Then tell me. Why did they have to leave? What do you have to say to me?"

He drew in a breath. His bracing to say whatever he had to made it harder for her to breathe herself. "A few things happened while you were at work."

Her eyes widened.

"Nothing to really worry about." He rushed to assure her. "Just some changes to the status quo."

"Okay." She was finding it hard to wait for him to get to the point.

"Tito showing up at your place again today shows we need to continue to protect you."

"Yes." Her heart was pounding as he reminded her of what she already knew.

"I don't have confirmation yet, but there's a chance I might be called away soon so I won't be here to protect you. I'm worried you might not be able to stay on base while I'm gone."

"You've already done enough. I'll find someplace—"

"No. I'm not telling you I can't help you anymore. I'm trying, badly, to explain that I think I found a better way."

"How?"

He opened his mouth but hesitated. Blowing out a breath, he reached out with his other hand so he held both of hers in his. "Keep an open mind, but if I found a way for you to be able to stay on the base even if I'm gone and a way for you to not have to worry about your visa or being deported, would you consider it?"

"Yes. Oh my God, of course." For the first time in days, he was giving her hope.

"Even if the way to do that was for us to get married?" He cringed.

"Married?" She widened her eyes. "You'd be willing to marry me just to protect me and Lola?"

"Yes."

She didn't know what to say. What to think. It

was the kind of sacrifice that family and the closest of friends might do for someone, but he was neither.

"I'll understand if you say no." Rocky began to ease his hands away from hers.

She grabbed on to his and held tight. "I'm not saying no."

He bobbed his head to one side. "You haven't said yes either."

With the shock of what he'd suggested, she was happy she was still able to form a sentence, never mind make a decision.

"Are you sure about this?" she asked.

"I wouldn't have brought it up if I wasn't."

Her heart fluttered like butterfly wings against the confines of her ribcage. "So we'd get married and then what?"

"Then we'd have the breathing room to straighten everything out."

"And you're really okay with that?" she asked, still in shock.

"Yes."

Isabel blew out a breath. "Then okay. Yes."

He smiled. "Good. It's settled then."

"She said yes!" Darci's exclamation was muted by the door until it slid open.

She'd obviously been watching through the glass, but now she burst through, Thom directly behind her.

Isabel noticed Jon and Ali stayed on the deck, deep in conversation once the door closed again. It was an interesting group. "I guess I get all of them as part of the deal."

Rocky's smile turned into a laugh. "Seems so.

For better or worse."

She couldn't be upset about that. It had been too long since she'd felt like she belonged somewhere. Since she had a family.

"So when are you going to do it?" Thom asked.

"I don't think we can get a license or a judge to marry us tonight. It'll have to be tomorrow, I guess." Rocky shrugged.

Thom lifted a brow. "It might have to be quick if it's tomorrow."

"Yeah. I know." Rocky raised his gaze to hers. "I'll explain more later, but sometimes we get shipped out pretty fast."

Thom snorted. "That's putting it mildly."

Rocky drew in a big breath through his nose. "Whatever happens, we'll deal with it."

"And I'm here. And Ali." Darci smiled at Isabel. "We'll help you."

"You're all so nice. I don't know how to thank you." The tears that had been building up over the day spilled out.

As Darci grabbed the tissue box from the kitchen counter and handed it to Isabel, the front door swung open and Chris, in a sweat-stained T-shirt, stepped into the room.

He looked from Isabel to Darci and frowned. "What did I miss? Why is she crying?"

"We're getting married." Rocky answered for them both. While she wiped her eyes, Isabel was happy to let him.

When Chris appeared at a loss for words at that information, Darci said, "They're happy tears."

"Oh, well that's good to hear." He reached out

and reeled Darci in for a hug.

Darci wrinkled her nose. "You're sweaty."

"Yup. I went for a run so I could check out the neighborhood without raising any notice." Chris captured her in a double-armed hug and pulled her closer as he asked, "So when's the wedding?"

"Hopefully tomorrow," Rocky answered.

"So soon?" Chris's brows drew low.

"We got a text. Unscheduled team meeting at zero-seven-hundred."

What Thom said had Chris nodding. "Ah. Gotcha."

"So I'll have to get a license and find someone to marry us tomorrow right after the meeting. Unless you happen to know a clerk and a judge who works Sunday nights." Rocky laughed.

"Actually, I might be able to help with that." Chris grinned.

Darci pulled back. "Seriously?"

"Yup. I got connections, darlin'. You impressed?"

"Yes, but I'll be more impressed after you shower and change clothes." Darci finally extricated herself from his sweaty hold, but softened the blow by pressing a kiss to his cheek. "Love you anyway."

"Love you too, darlin'." Chris turned to Rocky. "And if I can arrange for the license, I bet the base chaplain would be happy to get you two hitched tonight given the circumstances. Then you can at least have a wedding night. Right?"

Rocky laughed at Chris's comment and accompanying wink and then, sobering, cut his gaze to Isabel. "He's joking. We really just need the legalities out of the way so it's official."

"Yeah. The legalities. Mm, hm." Chris grinned wide.

Darci delivered a backhanded slap to Chris's midsection. "Leave them alone and stop teasing."

"You're no fun." Grinning, Chris slipped his cell out of a pocket in his shorts. "I'll go make some phone calls and see what I can do about a license."

"I'll give the base chaplain a call and see if he'd be willing to help out tonight. My ex-wife and I went to him for counseling before the divorce, so he knows me."

"You mean he *owes* you." Chris laughed. "Seems that counseling didn't work out so well."

As the guys continued to joke, Darci came to sit next to her. "So what are you going to wear for the ceremony?"

Isabel hadn't even considered what to wear for the wedding. She was far too preoccupied thinking about the wedding night.

CHAPTER FOURTEEN

"You all right?" Jon asked.

Rocky's heart thundered as he answered, "Yup."

Standing in front of the altar in the chapel on base waiting for his bride-to-be and the chaplain to arrive had made things start to feel really real.

His nerves must have shown. Jon eyed him critically. "You sure you're okay?"

"Yeah." Rocky took a closer look at Jon and the dark circles under his eyes. "Are you okay?"

Jon let out a short laugh. "If Ali doesn't kill me in my sleep tonight, yeah, I'll be fine."

"I noticed that long discussion out on the deck." Rocky had planned to not ask about it, but since Jon had brought up the subject himself . . .

"Yeah, that little talk was thanks to you." Jon lifted his dark brows.

"Me? Why me?"

"You've known Isabel for two days and you

asked her to marry you."

"And you know why."

"Yes, I do. And so does Ali, but it didn't seem to make any difference. The fact is we've been dating for years and she's not wearing a ring yet."

"Didn't you just ask her to move in? One step at a time, right? You move in together, then you get engaged, then you get married." It seemed to Rocky moving in together should have kept Ali happy for at least a little while.

Jon sighed. "Yes, and one day yeah, that's going to happen, but things are complicated right now."

And at that, Rocky decided to let the conversation go. He didn't need Jon's complications on top of his own. Right now he had to deal with everything he needed to do to prepare not only for possible deployment, but for leaving a brand new wife behind during it.

"Shit. I need to sign power of attorney over to Izzy before I leave. And I really should sign a new will leaving everything to her before I go."

Jon leveled a stare on Rocky. "You sure you want to do all that?"

"Yes. She needs the security more than my parents who own a frigging McMansion in New Jersey."

"McMansion?" Jon asked.

"Yeah. You know those huge houses they build in those developments where all the homes look exactly alike? Supersized and mass produced, like a Big Mac at McDonalds."

"Ah. Okay." Jon laughed.

"The point is my parents don't need to inherit

what little I have if I should get killed in action. But it could mean everything to Izzy and Lola's future."

Rocky's brain spun with trying to figure out how to do everything in so short a time. "I don't have a printer in my room and I won't have time to run to Legal—"

"I'll grab Thom and have him come with me to the GAPS office. I can print out the forms you need there and Thom can bring them to you at the meeting in the morning to sign. You should probably be able to find a notary on base. There are usually a few on staff at the bank. If you don't have time for that, just have a few of the guys sign and witness it and it'll be good enough."

It was a good plan. Yes, timing would be tight but he'd do what he had to do. "Thanks, Jon. But don't bother Thom. I can come with you to the office tonight."

Jon drew back at that offer. "No, you won't. I'm sure Thom won't mind. It'll take half an hour, max. Besides, you have a wife and a wedding night to get to."

Rocky rolled his eyes. "It's not going to be like that."

"Why not?"

"I just met her forty-eight hours ago."

"And?" Jon laughed.

Sighing, Rocky decided to not continue this conversation with Jon any further. Changing the subject, he glanced at the time on his cell phone, which hadn't left his hand since he'd left Izzy. "Where are they?"

"When I texted Ali, she said they were in the car

on their way over."

"I should have stayed with her."

"She's getting dressed for your wedding. Tradition says you seeing her is all sorts of bad luck."

"I think we're way past tradition here." Rocky sighed and checked the doorway again.

"Relax. Ali and Darci are with her for the girlie wedding stuff. Chris and Thom are both with her for protection, and Thom's got his ID to make sure they'll all get through the gate and onto the base without any delays. She's fine. You on the other hand, look like you need a drink."

Although that sounded like a really good idea right about now, he couldn't do it. "I'm not getting drunk for my wedding."

"You like her."

When Rocky looked up at Jon's odd comment, he found the man's gaze intent on him.

"Of course, I like her. So do you. She's a nice girl who doesn't deserve the bullshit she's going through."

"I think it's more than just that." Jon folded his arms and waited.

The silence grated on Rocky's nerves until he finally gave in. "Okay, yes. If she wasn't hiding from a crazy ex and facing possible deportation, and if I wasn't possibly shipping out to God only knows where tomorrow, yeah I'd probably ask her out. Go on a few dates. Get to know her better. What's wrong with that?"

Jon lifted one shoulder. "There's nothing wrong with that."

"There's just no time for that now with me possibly leaving."

"Mm, hm. I agree. It's not the wedding I'm questioning. It's your plans—or lack thereof—for the wedding night."

Before Rocky could tell Jon to mind his own business when it came to what did or did not happen on the wedding night, and that it wasn't really up to Rocky anyway because it took two to tango and he very much doubted Izzy would be up for any *dancing* with him tonight, Thom walked in.

He smiled as he approached. "Dude. You ready?"

Why did everyone keep asking him that?

"Yes." He tried to keep his frustration from seeping out in his answer.

"You got rings?" Thom asked.

Rocky mouthed a curse. "No. I didn't even think of rings."

"Then it's a good thing I came prepared." Thom reached into his pocket and pulled out two gold bands. One large. One small.

"Where'd you get those?" Jon asked.

"My room. I'm never going to use them again but I couldn't bring myself to throw them away. New England thriftiness, I guess." Thom delivered a crooked grin.

"So they're your divorce rings?" Rocky asked, staring at the two small circles in Thom's hand.

"There's no such thing as divorce rings. They're wedding bands that I no longer need because I'm divorced." Thom closed his fist around the rings in his palm. "But hey, you don't want them then—"

"No. I'll take them. Thank you." Rocky would take what he could get. "I'll buy new ones when I get a chance and give these back to you."

"Why bother? How long are you planning on staying married?" Thom asked.

It was a good question. One Rocky didn't have an answer to. "I don't know."

How long would things take to get straightened out? After they did, once Isabel wasn't in danger of being deported or harmed, it would make sense to dissolve the marriage.

The thought of a divorce or even an annulment didn't settle well with Rocky. And if the plan was to end the marriage, then of course he shouldn't be having the kind of wedding night Jon kept hinting at.

But what if he and Isabel hit it off? Would it be insane to stay married and see where things went?

He'd never been so confused in his life, which was probably why it took him this long to notice Thom was here alone.

Rocky frowned. "Where's Izzy? I thought you were with her."

Thom hooked a thumb toward the hallway. "Ladies room with Ali and Darci. She's feeding Lola."

And there was the other element that made this all the more confusing. Lola.

It honestly wouldn't bother him to raise another man's kid, but what would having Rocky in her life only temporarily do to Lola? Children needed stability in their family life.

Chris and Brody pushed through the doorway

wearing twin grins when they spotted Rocky.

The sight knocked him out of his worry and had him smiling. "Wow. Both Cassidy brothers are here. I'm honored."

"Hell, when Chris texted that one of my teammates was getting hitched, there was no way I was missing it." Brody laughed and dropped his gaze to take in the dress uniform Rocky had chosen to wear. "Looking good."

"Thanks." Rocky ran a finger between this collar and his throat.

The base chaplain had done them a huge favor in light of the situation and waived all the usual requirements, so Rocky figured he should show the man and the ceremony due respect and wear his dress uniform. Just because they were getting married in an unorthodox manner didn't mean he shouldn't look good.

But damn, had this damn thing always been so tight? Had his neck gotten thicker?

He didn't have much time to consider that. The door to the chaplain's office swung open and he walked out. "We all ready?"

Rocky turned to glance at the door of the chapel, looking to see if Isabel was there. "Um, she's—"

"She's ready." A smiling Darci opened the door as wide as it could go and secured it with the doorstop.

It took Rocky a moment to recognize the woman who stepped past Darci. Isabel was a vision of quiet beauty dressed in an off-white dress with a handkerchief bottom that swished around her ankles as she walked.

In her hand she held three pink roses tied with a white ribbon. The blooms matched the pink spots coloring her cheeks as her gaze met his.

He swallowed hard as she neared. This was it. No turning back now.

She held herself stiffly as she walked, her posture broadcasting she was battling nerves to rival his own. It was a reminder that they were in this together, for better or worse.

It made him want to comfort her. Reaching out, he slipped his hands palm up beneath hers. Darci jumped into action, stepping forward to take the roses so Izzy could lay her trembling hands in his.

Behind Darci, Lola babbled softly in Ali's arms as the small group of men Rocky had come to call friends surrounded her.

It twisted his heart that she didn't have friends of her own there. The only representative from her side was her daughter who was too young to remember this day.

That was all right. His friends would be her friends. They'd be there for her when he couldn't be, he was certain of that.

Just as his family would—

Crap! His parents.

He'd have to tell them something eventually. That was more than he could deal with before tomorrow's early morning meeting that could lead to him grabbing his kit and heading out.

His internal turmoil came to a halt as the chaplain, who'd been delivering words this whole time that Rocky couldn't absorb, looked directly at him and said, "Do you, Sylvester Anthony

Mangiano take Isabel Celeste Alvarez to be your lawfully wedded wife?"

As the vow he was about to make stole the breath from his lungs, Rocky heard what sounded like Chris say, "Sylvester? That's his name?"

At that shocked comment, someone else Rocky couldn't see because they were behind him snorted out a laugh.

The interaction added some much needed comic relief to the situation whose seriousness was threatening to make Rocky have to puke behind a pew . . . until he looked into her eyes.

There he saw the emotions roiling through her. Fear. Hope. Some of the same things he felt.

They'd face it all together.

Holding her trembling hands in his, Rocky squeezed her fingers and said, without a shade of doubt, "I do."

He watched her face as she kept her eyes on him through the chaplain's question to her and her response. "I do."

The chaplain's words continued in a blur until one sentence stood out from among the rest, "You may kiss the bride."

It was the easiest order he'd ever followed.

Rocky watched her eyes widen as he leaned in and pressed his lips to hers. He wanted to taste her mouth thoroughly and in private, but instead he had to deliver a kiss chaste enough to not offend the clergyman standing just a couple of feet away.

The applause of the small but enthusiastic crowd of onlookers was an additional reminder of the time, the place, the audience present for their first kiss.

Rocky did notice that at some point he'd ended up with his hands gripping her around the middle, as her hands ran up the front of his chest, stopping just below the rows of the ribbons he'd earned in service.

After one last squeeze of his fingers around her waist, he forced himself to break the kiss, saddened that it might have been the first and the last time for any sort of physical intimacy between them.

Pulling back he held his breath and sought to gauge her reaction from the expression on her face. There was surprise, which he didn't blame her for one bit. He was shocked as shit himself at how easily they'd fallen into the kiss.

But there was something else in her expression too. Something that gave him hope that maybe tonight, their first night alone together, wasn't going to be so awkward after all.

CHAPTER FIFTEEN

"So this is it. Our humble abode."

Isabel followed Rocky through the door and glanced around. She hadn't known what to expect from the room he had rented on the base.

What she got was a space twice the size of what she'd expected, since it was two rooms actually.

She moved into the living room, decorated with a small sofa and chair, coffee table and lamp. It was outfitted with a kitchen area that included a fridge, sink and microwave, and even a small dining table with two chairs.

Just past the built-in wall shelves was a doorway to the bedroom. Through the open door she could see the one big bed.

Yes, she'd had a child, but she'd only been with one man in her life. Tito. The result was asleep in the car seat carrier that Rocky stood holding now.

He looked around the room and finally stepped

toward the low, wide cocktail table. After setting the carrier down, he turned to face Isabel.

"When I checked in I requested a crib for her." He glanced at the bedroom door. "If it's not here yet, I can run down to the front desk and check on it."

Once she could drag her attention off the single large bed, she spotted the crib up against the wall next. "It's in there."

"Oh, good. Then we're set." He looked as unsure of what to do next as she did. "I guess we should put her to bed in it?"

Isabel smiled. "Or we could leave her there until she wakes up. Then after I feed her I'll put her down in the crib."

"Let sleeping babies lie. Got it." He gazed at Lola, looking like an angel in sleep, then he turned to Isabel. "I'll learn. I promise."

It struck her exactly how much Rocky was taking on to help her. A wife. A child. The whole mess with Tito.

She raised her eyes to meet his gaze. "Thank you."

He lifted a brow. "For what?"

She shook her head. "For everything."

It had been a long and event-filled day, which she'd navigated on the heels of a night where she didn't get nearly enough sleep. It all combined to make her super emotional now.

Her lip was trembling, so she bit down on it and tried not to cry.

He was in front of her in two long strides, the weight of his hands on her shoulders. "Don't.

You're safe here. Tomorrow I'll apply for family housing on base. Now that we're married you'll be a priority for temporary lodging until they assign us something permanent."

She couldn't keep track of all the details, of all the plans he was laying out for her. All she could absorb was the feeling that he was handling everything to insure her and Lola's safety.

The tears overflowed her eyes.

"Come here." He pulled her to him, enveloping her in the warmth of his arms.

She was pressed against a man she didn't even know a few days ago, but it didn't feel odd.

It felt good. Safe. Right.

Isabel wrapped her arms around his waist and held tight. He responded by leaning his head against the top of hers and rubbing his hands up and down her back.

The touch spread the warmth of his embrace. It penetrated the cold chill of fear, replacing it with a feeling of comfort.

Being in Rocky's arms cut through her fear as it also sliced through her defenses.

She thought she'd never trust a man again after Tito . . . until Rocky.

Unlike Tito, Rocky didn't just tell her to blindly trust him. Rocky showed her she could count on him by his actions. Proved it with his quiet support. With a dozen little things he did, from bringing her food to opening her door, to remembering to ask for a crib for Lola.

And now they were married—his biggest sacrifice of all and he dove head first into the decision, seemingly without any doubt or second thought.

She was his wife in the eyes of God and the law. And now she realized she wanted to be his wife in practice as well as name.

Isabel leaned back and tipped her head back to be able to see his face above hers. She leaned closer and lifted up on her tiptoes.

His eyes widened with surprise for the briefest of moments before they narrowed again. He drew in a breath that had his chest rising beneath her splayed palms.

She couldn't quite reach his mouth. He was taller than she was, even in the heels Darci had insisted she wear for the ceremony with the dress she'd loaned her. But it was obvious he understood what she was aiming for.

He dipped his head lower and held there, letting her close the final distance.

His beard was so much softer than she'd imagined it would be. A small part of her brain had registered that during the ceremony, but that kiss had been so overwhelming she hadn't thought too much about it.

Here, alone with him on their wedding night with her lips pressed to his she absorbed the sensation. The feel of his beard against her skin.

Soft. Smooth. Pliable.

Nothing like the closely cropped facial hair, more like long razor stubble, that Tito wore. His rough hair had scraped her raw, leaving the skin around her mouth red and chafed.

Then again, Tito's kisses were rough too. He was

nothing like Rocky gently working her mouth with his now.

She shouldn't be comparing the two men. Especially not now on their wedding night, but she couldn't help it. The differences were so glaring.

It was a good kiss. The best she'd ever had, and she wanted more. She ran the tip of her tongue against his lips, just for a second.

Rocky groaned deep and low in his throat. He angled his head and plunged his tongue against hers, kissing her with more enthusiasm but still just as gently.

His hands roamed her body while his mouth was on hers. It all caused a deep need that twisted inside her.

The uniform he wore was a barrier between her and his body, but pressed this closely to him she could feel that he had the same need.

They made out right there, standing in the middle of the living area of the hotel room he'd rented to keep her safe, just as how he'd married her for the same reason.

It had been so long since she'd felt even the tiniest bit secure that feeling it now was like a drug.

Her problems weren't solved. The Tito situation wasn't over. But for right now, she was safe.

Cloistered away on a Navy base where men in uniform manned the gate with automatic weapons Tito couldn't get to her. And even if he did get on the base somehow, she was with Rocky. He would do anything to protect her. He'd already proven that today when he'd said *I do*.

It was dizzying. Euphoric. She wanted to live,

feel, embrace life . . . and him.

That desire translated into her attacking Rocky like she was a starving woman. Maybe she was. Starved for love. Affection. Physical pleasure that she hadn't even thought about for the year she'd been in hiding.

She kissed him harder. Deeper. With a desire she didn't know she could feel. She was gasping, her heart pounding, her blood racing through her veins by the time she broke the kiss so she could breathe.

He leaned his forehead against hers and sucked in a lungful of air, blowing it out between his lips.

Bringing his hands up to cup her cheeks, he pulled back to gaze down at her and waited. Waited for her to make the next move . . . or not. She knew without him saying it that the choice was hers.

For the first time, she felt in control of the situation. Something she'd never felt with Tito.

Though that presented a problem in itself. If she wanted to be with Rocky, she'd have to tell him. That was a nerve-wracking concept.

"Do you want to go to the bedroom?" She forced herself to meet his gaze.

He didn't answer. Instead Rocky reached down and scooped her up. He'd taken a single step toward the bedroom when he stopped. Turning with her in his arms, he looked back at Lola, still sound asleep in the car seat. "Can we leave her there?"

"Yes. If the door's open I'll hear her."

Her affirmation was all it took for Rocky to spring into action, striding across the room toward the bedroom. He only slowed down long enough to turn sideways so they could fit through the doorway, then he resumed the fast pace to the bed.

Braced on one knee, he laid her on top of the bedspread and then stood to gaze down at her. "You're sure about this?"

Maybe it was crazy, but no more so than the fact they were married. It could all be temporary, dissolved the moment her problems were solved, but for right now she was completely certain. She wanted this.

"Yes." She nodded.

He let out a burst of air, as if he'd been holding his breath waiting for her answer. Then he reached for the buttons of his uniform.

Piece by piece the uniform came off, exposing another part of her husband to view.

Her *husband.* The word felt strange to even think. She had yet to say it aloud.

She watched as he slowly stripped off the formal vestiges of his career until just the man stood before her. He was as glorious unclothed as she imagined he would be.

In nothing but navy blue underwear, he reached one hand to her. Isabel took it and felt the strength of his grip as he pulled her upright.

After swinging her legs over the side of the bed, she stood on unsteady limbs. She rested her hands on the dusting of dark hair that covered the hard muscles of his chest.

She didn't get to spend nearly enough time touching him before Rocky turned and reached for the bed covers.

He made short work of flipping back the bedspread and sheets. Then with the same quick efficiency, did the same to strip her, lifting the dress up and over her head.

Instead of her usual ugly beige nursing bra, for the wedding Isabel had had to wear one of her pre-baby bras because of the cut of the dress. Her breasts popped out of the top of it but she was grateful for the pretty lace of the bra now as she stood before him in nothing but heels and lingerie.

He reached for her and pulled her toward him. The first feel of his hands against her bare skin had her sucking in a sharp breath. Then her mouth was covered again by his as he backed her up until her knees hit the edge of the mattress and buckled.

She half sat, half fell onto the bed. He left her sitting there to stride across the room to a duffle bag she hadn't noticed before. It sat on the floor next to her suitcase. He must have brought their bags inside when he'd checked in before the ceremony. While she'd been getting dressed at Darci's house.

Her train of thought regarding luggage came to a screeching halt when he pulled a small black bag out of the duffle, and out of that emerged with what seemed like a very long strip of condoms.

With the sound of her pulse thundering in her ears, she watched as he went to the other side of the bed and climbed in.

She remembered she had her shoes on and slipped the heels off, letting them drop to the floor before she swung her bare feet onto the bed and slipped them beneath the turned down sheets.

He waited for her to roll so she was on her side facing him before he edged closer and laid a hand on her hip. Lying on his side mirroring her position, he waited.

The silence got to her quickly and she felt the need to fill it. "I'm nervous."

He let out a short laugh. "So am I."

Isabel swallowed. "What should I call you?"

"Anything you want. What do you want to call me?"

She'd heard his given name during the ceremony, but Sylvester seemed so foreign after knowing him as Rocky since meeting him. And it seemed too soon for any other endearment. The American *honey*. The Latino *amorcito*. She silently rehearsed different ones in her head and none felt right.

"Rocky, I guess."

"Then call me Rocky."

She dropped her gaze to the very small distance separating their bodies. The space made smaller by the protrusion of his erection tenting his briefs.

"Even during?" At her question, he laughed full out.

"*During* you could probably call me anything and I wouldn't care." He sobered. "You know you're not obligated to me in any way. Don't feel like you have to do this as some sort of payment or thanks."

"I don't feel that way."

"No? You sure about that?" he asked, looking doubtful.

"Yes." She wiggled closer so she and he were nose to nose. "I'm very sure."

He swallowed hard as his gaze dropped to her lips. "Good."

There was no more talking as he drew in a breath and pressed his mouth to hers. This time there were no clothes between them, just the lace of her underwear and the cotton of his. Neither provided much of a barrier as he hauled her hips against his.

He ran his hand down between them, slipping it beneath the top of her panties and then lower. She couldn't stop the sound of pleasure that escaped her when he connected with her core.

Groaning, Rocky broke the kiss.

"Yes." He delivered the single breathy word as his hand on her had her lifting her hips toward him, seeking more.

He gave her what she needed.

The sensations building inside her combined with the intimacy of his softly whispered encouragement close to her ear.

Feeling the need for something to hold on to she reached for him but her fingers couldn't wrap around the bulge of his biceps. Raising her gaze to his face, she found his heavily lidded brown eyes focused solely on her.

When their eyes met, his lips parted. He leaned closer and took her mouth. The plunging of his tongue between her lips combined with the feel of his fingers between her legs had her careening toward untold pleasures.

Gasping for breath she tipped over the edge of control and into the abyss where her world narrowed to nothing but Rocky and what he made her body feel.

She was aware of his softly shushing her followed shortly by the sound of Lola's cries.

The sound brought her back down to earth, fast and hard.

Horrified, she turned to Rocky, wide-eyed. "Oh my God. I woke her up. I'm a horrible mother."

He sounded as breathless as she was as he laughed. "No, you're not. You just got a little loud."

She kicked at the sheets to untangle her feet. Shame had her pushing away from him so she could get to the baby screaming in the next room.

The next room!

She must have been loud to have woken Lola from that distance. Yes, the door had been left open at her request, but still . . .

Striding barefoot across the bedroom carpet she remembered she was in nothing but a bra and underwear as the cold air of the room brushed over her bare skin.

While unbuckling the squirming child, Isabel vowed her time for being selfish was over. It was time to be a mother again.

"Come here. It's okay." She looked around the room. For lack of a better place, she sat on the hard cushion of the sofa.

She was just lifting her breast out of the scratchy lace and missing the convenience of her nursing bra when Rocky came through the door.

"Um. Here. I brought you this. It's chilly." Avoiding looking at her chest, he draped a blanket over her.

"Thank you."

Pausing for a second, his gaze dropped to the baby, nursing happily, before he yanked his focus up to her face. "Um, I'll give you some privacy."

"You can stay. It's all right."

"You sure?"

"Yes." She reached for the edge of the blanket covering the sofa next to her. "Sit."

"Okay." He did as she said, flipping the corner of the blanket over his lap.

She wasn't sure if that move was to guard against the temperature of the room, or his attempt to cover his underwear—or rather what was outlined within.

Now she'd given him permission to stay, he didn't avert his eyes. Instead he watched Lola and smiled. "She's a good eater."

Isabel smiled too. "She sure is. Thank God I can breast feed or she'd bankrupt me in the cost of formula."

"About that. Tomorrow we'll get you your military spouse ID. Then you can come and go through the gate without any issues and you can shop for food at the commissary here on base. The prices are much cheaper than out in town."

"Oh, okay."

"And if I'm not here to show you around, I'll get the Family Readiness Group people to stop by."

She glanced at him. "I can just wait until you get off work tomorrow."

He inhaled and let it out. "That's the thing. I might not be coming home tomorrow. I could be flying out and I never know when I'll be back, so don't wait. I can ask Jon or somebody else to show you around if you don't want to deal with the FRG but please let someone help you. There's a lot to do and to learn. I don't want you struggling through it on your own. Okay?"

Over the past day she'd gotten hints about his job in the military and what effect it could have on them, but this was the first time it really started to sink in. He could really be gone tomorrow and she'd be alone in a strange place.

It wouldn't be the first time, but she'd already been through that stage once in this town. The way he was setting her up for being without him, it was looking very real that he was leaving.

"Promise me that you'll accept help." He pinned her with a stare.

With an uncomfortable feeling of dread inside her, she nodded. "Okay. I promise."

"Thank you." He went silent as she moved to switch Lola to the other breast, containing her smile as his eyes stayed glued to the process and his mouth hung open with fascination.

He swallowed so hard when the baby latched on she could hear him. He seemed torn, like he didn't know whether to run away or watch. As off kilter as she felt about everything that had happened lately, it was oddly nice to see him uncomfortable too.

It wasn't too much longer until Lola had her fill. Her tiny eyelids fluttered and finally dropped.

"Is she sleeping?" Rocky whispered.

"Yes."

"She's still . . . um . . . attached." He glanced at where the baby remained latched on to her nipple and cringed. "What are you going to do?"

"Watch." Isabel wet her index finger and slid it between Lola's mouth and the nipple until it broke the suction and the baby popped off. Lola didn't move, but kept on sleeping like an angel. "See?"

He drew in a breath and let it out. "Yup. I saw."

As she wiggled to the edge of the sofa while cradling the sleeping baby in her arms, he stood and the blanket fell away from his lap.

With him standing and her still seated, she couldn't help but notice the situation in his briefs hadn't changed. If anything, it had gotten more pronounced.

Now that the baby was sleeping again, Isabel wouldn't mind returning to where they'd left off. Judging by the looks of him, he was ready for the same thing.

"I'm going to put her down in the crib. Then we can go back to bed . . . if you want to."

A narrowing of his eyes and a sharp intake of breath that flared his nostrils wide preceded his nod. "Yeah. I want to."

CHAPTER SIXTEEN

Rocky followed Isabel into the bedroom, torn as to what to feel.

There was his peaceful admiration of the serene beauty of the maternal scene playing out in front of him as Isabel laid the sleeping babe in the crib. The babe he'd taken on as his responsibility today.

Then there was the raging hard-on he couldn't seem to control around his new wife even at the most inappropriate of times, such as now. All she'd done was feed Lola but the scene had him crazed.

To be fair, he wouldn't have had to control his lust if they'd finished what they'd started. They'd both been yanked from bed at the most inopportune time—for him anyway.

This was what it was like to have a child and he didn't resent Lola for waking. Not one bit . . . but he was sure happy she was sleeping again. And he was definitely ready to get back to what he and Izzy had been doing before the baby woke.

When Isabel turned to him, arms empty of the child, Rocky saw the path to his satisfaction was clear. He stepped forward and closed the distance between them.

Sliding his hands around her waist, he connected with her warm bare skin.

Time to get this wedding night back on track. He lifted her until her feet were off the ground and crashed his mouth against hers.

Blind as he carried her, he walked them both toward the bed.

His bare foot landed on one of her shoes. As the pain shot through the sole he fell, tumbling them both onto the mattress.

She squealed beneath him. He cringed and held his breath, waiting to see if they'd disturbed the baby.

When no sound came from the crib behind him, he turned his focus back to Isabel. "You okay?"

"Yes."

It wasn't lost on him how perfectly they were aligned. Face to face. Her beneath him. His length nestled in the warm V between her legs.

Her lips were plump and perfect, inviting his kiss. He accepted the invitation.

Lowering his mouth to hers, he kissed those tempting lips. He plunged inside the heat of her mouth, tangling his tongue with hers. Stroking into her until he was groaning and breathless.

It hadn't taken very long for it to become very obvious that a kiss, no matter how good it was, was not nearly enough to slake his need for her.

If he could magically make their underwear disappear his happiness would be complete. He'd be plunging inside this woman in seconds.

As it was, his hips seemed to have a mind of their own as he ground against her beneath him.

The reality was he didn't have the superpower to make panties disappear. And he needed to get to the condoms on the nightstand.

Letting out a breath to restore some small amount of control, he rolled off her. He walked around the bed and took care of the protection issue.

When he turned back to face her, he saw she'd taken off the final barrier and was stretched out completely naked and waiting for him. He wouldn't make her wait long.

Rocky was across the mattress and on top of her quicker than he'd cleared the razor wire during his last timed run on the obstacle course.

This feat of speed and dexterity was far better than that team training would ever be because it led him to what he wanted so badly it hurt. Izzy.

He was all for foreplay, but he'd waited long enough already to get here and he wasn't about to postpone the main event any longer. He nudged between her legs and watched her eyes drift shut as she pressed her head back into the pillow.

Her open-mouthed intake of breath as he pushed farther into her wet heat cut straight through any control he'd managed to hold on to. He could be gone in the morning, sent he didn't know where or for how long. He gave them both what they needed. Hot. Hard. Sex.

Rocky didn't let himself think about the many

questions that hung over them. There'd be plenty of time when he couldn't be with her to obsess over their future, her past, the present danger.

He'd have hours on the transport and during down time on the mission he was likely going on. But now, they were here together and his brain was having trouble thinking about anything other than how incredible it felt to finally be inside the woman he'd wanted since the first time he'd touched her. Back when they'd been not much more than strangers.

Eyes closed, he absorbed every sensation, committing it to memory for when they were apart.

With the bulk of his weight braced on his arms, he took what he needed with back-bowing thrusts that rocked them both and the bed until the headboard slammed against the wall.

He bit back a curse and held still, glancing toward the crib to see if the noise had woken the baby.

"She's okay." Isabel reached down and pulled him closer. Deeper.

Sliding his hands beneath her, he lifted her hips off the bed and plunged in again and again and she met him stroke for stroke.

His wife was proving to be an equal match for him in the bedroom. He could definitely handle that.

The realization that this was a marriage of convenience and wouldn't last forever niggled uncomfortably at the back of his brain. But as an orgasm rocked him with the intensity of a fireworks factory exploding he couldn't think of a single reason to ever end this marriage.

CHAPTER SEVENTEEN

"Shit." The moment Rocky opened his eyes and saw the sunlight coming through the blinds he knew he was late.

"What's wrong?" Sleepy and warm and too soft and comfortable to sleep next to—which is why he was going to be late for the meeting—Isabel rolled toward his side of the bed.

Rocky paused only long enough to press a hard kiss to her mouth before he hopped up. "I slept late."

On his way to the bathroom, he frowned at the crib. "How come she didn't wake up? I thought she ate like every three hours or something, so I didn't set an alarm."

He was multitasking—peeing in the toilet while running the hot water in the shower—when he heard Isabel laugh through the partially open door.

"You never count on a baby to stick to a schedule."

Lesson learned. He only hoped he'd be back here to sleep tonight so he could put his new knowledge to good use. Though he was having trouble feeling too bad about having slept late since it happened because of some kick ass sex. Twice, because once hadn't been enough.

Hell, last night he'd been like a teenager again, sporting a perpetual erection. Even now, rushing and running late he had a semi-hard-on.

No time for that. He wished he did but as it was, he was already going to slide into the meeting with not a minute to spare *if* he was lucky.

If there was something up and a mission was in the works, he didn't think Grant was going to give him a pass for being late, wedding night or not.

He showered and brushed his teeth as fast as he could get the job done and was just toweling off when he caught sight of his wife. Naked. Bending over to open her suitcase.

And there was that erection again.

Shaking his head, he drew in a breath and chomped down on his desire.

God help Grant if he'd called this early meeting for no good reason because Rocky wanted nothing more than to sink into this woman one more time and then follow that up with a nice big breakfast.

Izzy pulled out a T-shirt and had just slipped it over her head, covering a few of his favorite parts, when Rocky made a decision.

How mad would Grant be if he were ten minutes

late? At least he could take care of one of his needs. He strode to her and slipped his hands around her waist from behind.

"I didn't give you a proper good morning."

She laughed, most likely because his erection was poking her in the back. "Good morning to you too. I thought you were late."

"Eh, just a little." Nuzzling her neck he glanced past her at the clock. He was just trying to judge how fast he could be when Lola made her presence known. He drew in a breath and released his hold on Izzy.

"Sorry." She glanced over her shoulder at him as she strode toward the crib.

"No. It's good. Saved by the baby." He reached into his duffle and grabbed a clean pair of briefs. After pulling them on, he followed her and smiled as Izzy lifted his new stepdaughter out of the crib. "Next time, I need the wake up call closer to zero-six-hundred. Okay, little girl?"

"I'll add that to her schedule." Isabel's lips tipped up and Rocky realized how much more she smiled now.

She could relax knowing she was safe here on base. If nothing else this marriage had removed the worry and stress she'd carried for so long.

The bed was a mess and the room smelled like sex, evidence that this marriage meant more than just making her safe. So much more . . .

And he had to stop fucking around and get going or he'd be in trouble with command. The same logical voice in his head also reminded him that when he left this room, he might not be coming back for quite a while, if at all.

That knowledge added to the turmoil of the growing To Do list in his head. All the things he needed to take care of now they were married to make her official.

If things played out as he'd come to expect from this command, the team could have just hours to get their shit together and onto a transport. And those hours could be filled with running over the mission plan, studying locations, memorizing details, learning things about the target and site to give them the highest likelihood of success.

Then he needed time to get his kit. He always restocked it immediately upon returning from an assignment so he'd be ready to go again. But his basic set-up was usually in need of tweaking, time allowing, to meet any specific needs of the new assignment.

Crap. Too much to do—and so much more he simply wanted to do—with not nearly enough time to do it.

He grabbed Isabel and turned her to face him. Even with the baby in her arms he pressed a kiss to her mouth, and then brushed his lips lightly across the baby soft hair on the top of Lola's head.

"I really do need to run. If it turns out I'm getting sent right out today I probably won't have time to come back here first. But I'll call Jon and he'll make sure you are set up with anything you need. I'll make sure he has your cell number so keep it with you so he can call with the details."

She frowned not looking relieved at what Rocky had hoped would be an encouraging speech.

"Will you be able to call me?" she asked.

He drew in a breath and made a promise he only hoped he'd be able to keep. "Yeah. It might have to be quick, but I will call before I leave."

"Okay."

Her biting her lower lip with worry had his heart twisting, even as it made him want to suck that pouty lip into his mouth—along with a few other tasty parts of her.

Leaving her was going to be harder than he'd ever imagined.

He had to drive like a bat out of hell once he finally finished getting dressed and said goodbye to Izzy. He risked getting pulled over because of it, but luck was on his side and he made it without getting caught.

Rocky slid into the meeting room almost five minutes late. Lucky for him, Grant was later. Sure the team commander was probably in his office on the phone handling some important details, but the fact remained, Rocky was in his seat before Grant was in the room, and that was good enough for him.

Thom leaned back in his chair and folded his arms, eyeing Rocky. "You're late."

"I had to make sure Izzy was settled before I left."

"Mm, hm. I'm sure that's exactly what it was that had you running in late." Brody's comment came from the other side of Rocky.

The last thing he needed was his two teammates tag teaming him with questions about Isabel. Then again, he was in such a good mood he couldn't care what they said.

Bring it on. Thom's girl lived up north and Brody's girl was in Alabama, so it was safe to say of the three, Rocky had been the only one to get any last night.

That knowledge was enough to allow him to be magnanimous and tolerate the teasing. They were obviously jealous. And so they should be.

Rocky grinned but refused to give them the satisfaction of any further response, even when they both kept peppering him with questions and prods.

As the door opened and Mack slipped inside, silently taking his seat even later than Rocky had, there was finally something else for his two nosy teammates to focus on.

"You're late too. And where were you all weekend?" Brody asked frowning.

"Family stuff." Staring straight ahead, it was obvious that was all the response Mack was going to give.

He always had been a man of few words but that answer was short even for him.

Across the table Dawson, the newest guy on the team, watched all the interaction but kept his mouth shut.

Smart man. He'd learned quickly.

The door opened and Grant walked into the meeting room, ending any further conversation.

He tossed the file folders in his hand on the table and glanced at the team members gathered there. "I know we just got back and I expect there's probably gonna be grumbling on the home front that some of you unlucky bastards will have to deal with . . ."

That prelude to their orders was enough to sink

Rocky's hopes. He loved his job, but he would have loved it more if he'd had at least a few weeks before they shipped out again.

Not because he needed the rest between ops, but because Izzy needed him here. Hell, after one night with her, he was feeling pretty needy when it came to her as well.

"All I can tell you is this. This assignment? It's a good one." Grant grinned and Rocky's mood and his ears perked up.

He could only imagine what it would be and he sure as hell couldn't wait to hear.

CHAPTER EIGHTEEN

The first day of Isabel's married life had started early with her new—albeit temporary—husband running out the door just after sunrise to get to a meeting.

An hour later, it couldn't have been much longer than that, Lola was fed, bathed and dressed for the day and Isabel slowed down enough to realize she was getting pretty hungry herself.

The problem was, she didn't know what to do about that. She was just considering driving around the base in search of food when her cell phone rang.

"Hello?"

"Hey. It's Rocky."

"I know." She smiled. She'd recognize his voice anywhere. Especially after hearing it against her ear last night.

"I wasn't sure. Anyway, I can't talk long and I'm really sorry, I'm not gonna make it back to the room to see you. I'm about to board a plane."

Her smile disappeared. "Oh. Do you know when you'll be back?"

"No. But I'll call when I can."

"Okay." She didn't know what to say. There were so many things she needed to ask. More than she had time for.

She was trying to narrow the list down to the most important few things when he said, "Shit. Gotta go. Talk soon. Bye."

The click of his disconnecting came at the same time she said, "Bye."

She glanced around the room feeling alone and helpless. How long did she even have the room for? Was she supposed to stay until he got home or would she have to check out? And where would she go if she had to leave?

She didn't even have anyone's phone number.

Lola babbled, content on the blanket on the floor in the middle of her toys.

Isabel looked at her daughter, straightened her spine and renewed her resolve. They'd been in far more precarious situations than this. She could call the front desk and ask about the reservation. She had her car so she could drive to find something to eat.

They'd be fine. Heck, she didn't even need a phone number since she could drive over to Darci and Rick's house if she had to . . .

But if she left the base, could she get back on? And if she couldn't leave, would they allow her to buy food on base if she didn't have a military ID?

Every solution she thought she'd found seemed to raise a new question, another problem.

Things not looking as bright as she'd deluded herself into thinking, her determination waned.

Just as she was starting to panic all over again, her cell rang. She didn't recognize the number but dove for the button to answer it anyway, in case it was Rocky calling back from a different line.

"Hello?"

"Hey, it's Jon Rudnick. Rocky asked me to call."

"Jon. Hi. Thanks for calling." The relief flooded her. Giving up trying to be strong and upright, she sank down onto the sofa. "I have a few questions about some things."

That was the understatement of the day.

Jon's laugh came through the earpiece. "I'm sure you do. Don't worry. It'll take a bit of time but we'll get you all straightened out. I figure I'll grab Chris and come on over. We could be there in about an hour, if that works for you."

"That would be perfect."

"Good. The girls are working today but they wanted to do dinner with you tonight, if you're free."

Now it was Isabel's turn to laugh. What in the world else did she have to do? "Yeah. I'm free."

From there the ball started rolling and it hadn't stopped. Isabel did more in one day than she ever imagined possible.

Jon and Chris had proven Rocky had been correct in trusting them. She appreciated them and their military connections and knowledge more than she could express.

There had been a real chance things wouldn't go smoothly with Rocky being absent and the marriage certificate and power of attorney both signed yesterday. Isabel's requests had raised a few eyebrows.

Scrutiny of her was compounded by the fact she wasn't a citizen. She had last semester's college ID, a student visa that she hoped no one would check on because they'd find she had violated the terms by quitting school, a Cuban passport and a Florida driver's license.

Not exactly an impressive array of official identification.

The most valuable of all her assets were Rocky's friends. Jon and Chris countered every obstacle on her behalf. They went to battle for her using military-speak she had trouble even following.

By day's end she had her own military dependent photo ID they assured her would get her on base with no problem.

Of course that assurance was quickly followed by Jon's warning that she shouldn't leave the base alone and definitely not go to work until the Tito situation was straightened out.

The day wasn't all forms, lines and paperwork. There was also the tour of the base and everything on it and a rundown of the intimidating base rules and protocols.

By the time they'd met up with Ali and Darci for dinner, Isabel's head had been spinning.

Now, finally back in her hotel room, she laid an exhausted Lola in her crib and closed the door to the bedroom.

Darci was just wrenching the cork out of the bottle of wine they'd picked up when Isabel came out of the bedroom.

"You are drinking with us, right?" Darci asked putting the bottle down on the tiny counter. "You can pump and dump if you're worried about drinking while breastfeeding."

"Sure. Thanks." She wasn't much of a drinker but she felt like she needed it after today.

Ali opened the cabinet above the sink and took down three glasses. "This place is pretty nice."

"It is. I'd never been in these units before." Darci reached for the television remote control. "They even have a big screen TV."

Isabel hadn't had the experience of having adult girlfriends. She'd gone from her grandmother's home in Cuba, to a college dorm room, to being a single mother on the run.

Sitting on the sofa next to Darci while Ali poured the wine and they all talked was so normal it felt strange. As much as she enjoyed it, she reminded herself it was all temporary . . . just like the marriage to Rocky and when that went away, so would the friends that came with it.

When Ali handed Isabel the glass of wine, she took it and drank a long swallow.

The commercial on the television ended and a news program came on.

"In international news, a US special operations team killed the Islamic State's second-in-command in a pre-dawn raid early today inside Syria. Haji Imam, the ISIS finance minister, was the terror

leader considered the man most likely to take over for ISIS leader Abu Bakr al-Baghdadi, if he were captured or killed."

"We don't need to watch this stuff. Let's see if there's a movie on." Darci jumped from her seat on the sofa and reached for the remote control she'd set on the table.

Sitting in the one upholstered chair in the room, Ali yanked her gaze from where it had been glued to the story on the television. After shooting Isabel a sideways glance, Ali turned her attention to Darci, who was still standing and squinting at the remote control's many buttons in the room's dim light.

Meanwhile, the reporter on screen continued, "*Military sources say the terror leader was killed in a clandestine raid conducted on the ground by American special operations forces who entered Syria by helicopter. There had been hopes to take Imam alive but he and three others were killed in the firefight.*"

"I don't mind watching the news . . ." Isabel began her protest but Darci had already flipped to another station.

Why were Ali and Darci both acting so strangely, insisting on changing the channel? Why didn't they want her to see that news report?

"What's going on?" Isabel asked.

"What do you mean?" Darci didn't look at Isabel as her gaze stayed trained on the screen. "Oh, look. Meg Ryan. I know it's an old movie but I just love her in this one."

"Darci. Those special operations guys in Syria, was that Rocky's unit?" It sounded crazy even thinking it in her head. Saying it out loud had felt even more so, but in a way it made perfect sense.

Rocky suddenly getting shipped off on one hour's notice. How he wouldn't say where he's going. Then US forces are on the TV for killing a terrorist. All the pieces seemed to fit.

"The truth is, we don't know." Darci sat next to her, rubbing her back in what was probably meant to be a comforting action. No amount of back rubbing would quell the storm in her gut thinking that Rocky had been in Syria in a firefight.

"We'll never know. We're not allowed to know. Even after it's over." The frustration was clear in Ali's tone.

The late hour combined with Isabel's exhaustion amplified her fear. In a panic, Isabel angled to face Darci. "So then we need to watch the news. To see what's happening. To see if he's all right."

Darci had switched the channel before the report was complete. What if there had been US casualties?

"No." Darci shook her head. "That's a good way to drive yourself crazy. Besides, we don't even know it's his team. There are thousands of operatives, from all branches of service, at places all over the world. Rocky could just as easily be at a training here in the states."

Isabel didn't miss the fact she continued to keep possession of the remote control.

"Don't seek out the news, Izzy. I understand the impulse but believe me both Darci and I have been through this. It's too hard." Ali drew in a breath and let it out. "On you and on the relationship."

Isabel didn't know much about Ali and Jon but she did know about herself and Rocky. "There's no relationship. Rocky married me because of Tito and my visa issue."

Darci pinned her with a doubt-filled stare. "There are other ways to keep you safe. He didn't have to marry you. He wanted to."

"No. Really—"

Ali cocked a brow. "Izzy, Jon's condo is outfitted like a fortress. You could have hid out there and been more than safe, without being married to Rocky."

"I'm sure he just didn't want to put Jon out by asking if I could stay there. Just like how I felt bad inconveniencing Rick and Darci by staying at their place."

Darci pulled her mouth to one side. "Don't use us as an excuse. Rick's with Sierra most of the time and I had no problem sleeping at Chris's place. Nope. A man doesn't get married just to avoid inconveniencing his friends."

"I agree." Ali nodded, her gaze penetrating as she said, "Don't try and tell us you and Rocky aren't getting *closer.*"

"Well, I mean . . ." The blood rushing to her cheeks made Isabel give up trying to lie.

Darci's eyes widened. "Oh my God. Did you two . . . *have sex*?"

"Darci!" Ali squealed. "Don't ask that."

Isabel was ready to crawl under the sofa but definitely not to answer that question, even if the truth was she had jumped Rocky last night.

"Notice she didn't deny it." Darci smirked.

Still horrified at the turn the conversation had taken, Isabel couldn't control her smile. "All right. We kind of did."

"Kind of?" Ali asked, looking ready to bubble over with excitement. "Or did?"

Resigned, Isabel let out a huff. "Okay, we did."

The reaction from the two women in the room at that information had Isabel laughing full out. Prying friends or not, it was a good feeling to be able to laugh.

CHAPTER NINETEEN

The team transport touched down in Virginia barely forty-eight hours after they'd taken off.

In and out fast. That's what command wanted. Rocky too, truth be told, especially for this op.

Mission accomplished and now home to Isabel. He glanced at the time on his cell phone. It was too early in the morning to call and risk waking her. He could text Jon though and let him know he was home.

Not having any word from home was killing him.

While he'd been in the midst of the action he'd been fine, but after twelve hours in the air he was losing his mind not knowing how things went without him.

Rocky punched in a quick text to Jon and hit

send just as they popped the hatch.

Standing, he pocketed the phone and resolved himself to the knowledge he might have to wait until he'd stowed his stuff and drove to the hotel to find out anything.

And if for some reason Izzy wasn't in the same room?

Then he guessed he'd have to start making phone calls, no matter how early the hour, because he wasn't going to wait to find out where she was.

"Look who's in a hurry. I wonder why that is?"

Rocky was striding fast across the airfield in the dim pre-dawn light, loaded duffle on one shoulder when he heard Brody's smart ass comment behind him.

"Yeah, I see." Thom laughed behind him. "I don't have to wonder why and neither do you."

He didn't turn around. Didn't slow his pace. Rocky simply lifted his middle finger high in the air and kept walking. The sound of Thom and Brody laughing followed him all the way into the building.

Unloading, and then reloading and stowing his shit, always felt like it took forever. Today more than usual. But he worked his ass off to finish, in spite of the mocking of his teammates, and was pulling into the parking lot of the hotel before the sun rose over the building.

The hotel room he'd left her in days ago was on the second floor. He took the stairs two at a time, the key gripped tight in his hand. When he reached the door he held his breath and turned the key in the lock.

The base hotel wasn't like a real hotel. There

was no twenty-four hour clerk. The front desk was manned during business hours, and he was here way too early so he could only hope that Isabel was still in this room and not some stranger.

If someone new had checked in, they were sure going to get a surprise. With that fear firmly in mind, Rocky pushed the door open slowly.

The chain and the deadbolt weren't engaged. He'd have to yell at her about that later because no woman and child should be in a hotel alone—even on a military base—without dead bolting the door when they went to sleep.

She'd left the small light on over the sink—or at least he hoped it had been Isabel and not the new resident of this room.

Only one way to find out.

After closing the door softly behind him, he crept toward the bedroom.

He saw the crib first and breathed in relief. That was a good sign. Moving closer he smiled down at Lola, sleeping peacefully.

Relief washed over him. Where there was baby, there would be Mommy as well. Turning toward the bed he saw her beneath the covers.

He decided he would let her sleep a while longer as he showered but after that—once he'd washed the dirt of the past two days off him and crawled between those sheets next to her—all bets were off.

Rocky liked that plan.

Anticipation carried him to the bathroom and through showering and brushing his teeth.

Not bothering to put on clothes he slipped between the sheets naked. He slid all the way across the bed until he was up against the warmth of her body.

She rolled over and gasped when she saw him next to her.

"Good morning, beautiful." He brushed a hand across her cheek, pushing back the lock of dark hair that had fallen into her face.

"Oh my God. You're back." The final words were muffled as she threw herself against him and wrapped her arms around his neck. "Why didn't you call?"

"Plans weren't firm so I figured I'd surprise you."

The full truth was he wasn't allowed to tell her when he was coming home. Or where he'd been. Or why. And more than that, he knew too well that travel plans changed radically in the military.

She was too new to this world to understand all that.

"I was so worried." The pitch of her whisper rose and he heard the panic in it.

"Whoa. No need to get upset. I'm home safe and sound." He held her closer. Selfish bastard that he was, he loved the feel of her clinging to him.

"I saw a firefight on the news . . ." Her sentence trailed off.

"Do yourself a favor and don't watch, okay? The media get it wrong half the time anyway."

"I know I shouldn't. Darci and Ali told me the same thing." She dragged in a shaky breath. "I'm sorry. I'm better now."

"There's nothing to be sorry about. But, since you're better now . . ."

Izzy had such an effect on him he was already hard just from lying next to this woman.

His texts had loaded shortly after they'd touched down and there had been a day old message from Jon saying they'd gotten Isabel all set up on base. With that worry relieved, and Isabel in his arms, Rocky had other pressing needs.

He ran his hands down her body and groaned. "Damn, I missed you."

"I missed you too." She drew in a breath that filled her chest and had her nipples brushing against him through the cotton of her shirt.

That was enough to break his control.

For two days he wanted nothing but to come home to her. Over that time he'd found he liked the idea of having someone to come home to more and more.

And not just for the sex, though sex was certainly a bonus. That was proven when she reached between them and stroked him.

It would be nice to have her do that for an hour, or a lifetime, but he was too hyped up from the mission and from the need she instilled in him.

Pushing Isabel onto her back he slipped his hands beneath the bottom of the button-down nightshirt she wore.

He discovered she had on no underwear. Nothing beneath the shirt to impede his progress. No barrier to keep him from nudging between her legs.

It felt so good, so warm he couldn't stop himself. He slid inside.

"God, you feel good." He sucked in a breath, vowing he'd pull out and put on a condom.

In a minute.

Another few plunges inside her and not only was he gasping from the exertion as well as the overwhelming sensations assaulting him, but Izzy's breath was coming faster too.

As her muscles clamped down on his cock, there was no freaking way he was stopping until he felt her come around him.

Amid the thoughts buzzing in his brain, he was aware they needed to be quiet because the baby was sleeping, and that he needed to pull out or risk them having another kid.

Then it struck him. He wouldn't mind that. In fact, he wanted a baby with Izzy. Hell, more than one. Maybe four or even five.

He wanted Lola to have brothers and sisters and even cousins if his idiot little brother ever got his act together and settled down with one woman.

It was a discussion they'd have to have but now was not the time as she careened into an orgasm that rocked him to the core. Employing all of his self control, Rocky grit his teeth and held on tight as her body gripped his.

The second the pulsing of her climax slowed he pulled out and came with the intensity of pleasure denied and finally set free.

He realized he'd made a mess of her shirt but he couldn't feel all that bad about it. The damp cotton clinging to her stomach was nothing when compared to the enormity of his recent revelation.

Braced over her, his heart pounding not just from the sex, he said, "What if we stay married?"

Her mouth dropped open. "What?"

"I don't want a divorce or an annulment. I want you. And Lola." He laughed as a bubble of emotion overwhelmed him. The feeling of everything finally fitting into place in his life hit him full force. "I love you. Stay married to me."

He hadn't truly known it until he said it aloud but it was there, no doubt. Love like he'd never felt before.

"This is crazy, you know."

"Yup." His heart pounded as he waited for her answer.

Her eyes held his as tears glistened in them. "I love you too."

"So is that a yes?"

She let out a breathy laugh. "Yes."

Relieved, he kissed her hard.

Lola stirred in the crib, which reminded Rocky of his other coital revelation. He pulled back from her lips and said, "I want babies with you. Lots of them."

"Okay." She laughed.

Running his hands over her hips, he groaned at the thought of making those babies.

Smiling, Isabel struggled to sit up. "Can I take care of the baby we've got first before we get started on the next one?"

He sighed but couldn't control the smile as he teased her. "I guess so. Go ahead."

After a successful mission Grant had cut the team loose with a promise that barring any unforeseen incidents they'd all have leave for the next two days. Rocky intended to take full advantage of his time even if it meant ordering delivery and not stepping outside of this room.

He heard the text come through to his phone and smothered a curse. That's what he got for making plans.

As Isabel changed Lola's diaper, Rocky held his breath and reached for the cell on the nightstand. It wasn't from his command.

Letting out a shaky breath, he read the text from Jon.

Got news. Need to meet when you can.

Glancing at his wife as she tended to the baby he'd taken on as his own, Rocky typed in a reply.

Can it wait until tomorrow?

Roger. Call me when you're done with the honeymoon.

Jon's smart ass text had been signed with a winking emoticon.

Rocky didn't really care what Jon thought. All he knew was that reality and all of its problems would wait for another twenty-four hours. But his love for Isabel wouldn't have to.

CHAPTER TWENTY

Rocky glanced over to make sure Izzy and Lola were settled in the living room of the condo with Ali before he turned back to Jon. "Thanks for waiting for this meet."

"No problem. But I will say I'm happy you're finally back in society instead of holed up in your honeymoon suite. I've got some stuff coming to a head here that's going to require my undivided attention."

He wasn't going to apologize for enjoying what time he had with his new wife so instead, Rocky asked, "With GAPS?"

"Uh, yeah." Jon bobbed his head. "For the company and just a lot of stuff going on."

"That's great you guys are so busy."

The success of Jon's company gave Rocky hope

there was life after the teams. That had always been a concern of his. Now that he had a family, even more so.

"Yeah. It is good. So let's get down to business." Jon leaned forward. Rocky did the same. "Chris and I spent the day with Izzy on base while you were gone."

"Yeah, she told me. Thanks for that."

Jon waived away his gratitude. "No problem. I brought it up because while we were together, she told me quite a bit about Tito."

Rocky's gut clenched at just the mention of the man. "Okay."

"Apparently she was privy to quite a lot. The guy wasn't real discreet. She heard the names of his associates. Scheduled meeting times and places. Basically his entire operation."

Rocky leaned back. He saw where Jon was going with this and he didn't like it. Jaw clenched, he shook his head. "No."

"Hear me out—"

"I don't want her involved in any take down operation you have planned." Rocky kept his voice low so Isabel wouldn't hear, but he spoke firm enough Jon would know he wasn't playing around.

Making Isabel a sacrificial lamb was not an option.

"That's what I'm trying to tell you. She won't have to be involved. Thanks to Rick's connections in Miami, we were able to anonymously drop just enough information to the right people that the Feds are now setting up their own sting without Izzy's involvement. She won't be connected to it at all.

There's a trail a mile wide to follow and plenty of evidence for them to discover all on their own."

Rocky drew in a breath. "You certain it can't come back on her?"

"I am."

"Okay." Rocky blew out a huff of air, finally able to breathe again. "Thank you."

Jon laughed. "For that? That was nothing. Rick did most of the work. But here's the rest and this you do owe me big time for."

"What's that?" Rocky's guard was back up once again.

"I moved into Izzy's apartment while you were gone."

"Okay. And?"

"And he showed up, just like I expected."

Hissing in a breath, Rocky cut his gaze to Izzy to make sure she was still occupied before saying, "No surprise there, I guess."

"Nope. The only surprise was his when I opened the door." Jon smiled.

"And how'd that go?"

"Pretty good. I went all out. Cardboard moving boxes broken down and stacked outside for recycling. More moving boxes inside. Newspaper and stuff all over the apartment like I was in the middle of unpacking. I answered the door in my underwear with a beer in my hand. It looked pretty convincing if I do say so myself."

Rocky lifted his brow. "Yeah. I'd say so. So what did he say?"

"He said he was looking for the woman who lived there. I played dumb and said I'd just moved in, but that the landlord had told me his last tenant had taken all her stuff and skipped out on her lease without any notice. The beauty is, that's pretty much the truth."

Rocky shook his head. "Wow. You're good. You think he bought it?"

"Judging by his cussing and storming away, I think he did. I wouldn't move her back into the apartment though, just in case."

"Yeah. About that . . . " Time for the big reveal. "We're gonna do this. Izzy and I are going to stay married. Live on base. Have more kids."

Rocky finally lifted his eyes to meet Jon's gaze.

The man was grinning. "I had a feeling that was where you were headed."

"Really? Because I'm not even sure I knew where this was going until yesterday."

Jon lifted one shoulder. "Sometimes it's harder to see what's close to us. You needed a little distance."

"Yeah. Guess so." Syria had sure provided plenty of distance. But it was the feeling of coming home to Izzy that had clinched it for him. He wanted that feeling every day for the rest of his life. "So anyway, I called and confirmed we're on the list for our permanent housing assignment and I'm planning on going to Legal to see about adopting Lola."

Jon smiled. "I'm happy for you guys."

"Thanks. And just so you know the water's fine, in case you're thinking of taking the plunge yourself." Rocky kept his voice low so the girls wouldn't hear.

Even so, Jon shot a quick glance at Ali in the living room before answering, "I got a few things to straighten out first."

"All right. I hear ya." Rocky kept any further comment on the matter to himself.

He turned to glance toward the living room. Izzy caught his gaze and smiled. He couldn't have controlled his own smile if he'd wanted to.

"So, you tell your parents yet that you got married and got yourself a kid all without telling them?"

Rocky leveled a glare at Jon as the man yanked him back to reality. "No, not yet. And thanks for reminding me."

"Anytime." Jon grinned. "That's what friends are for."

The tinkling sound of Isabel and Ali laughing in the living room caught his attention. She looked so happy she was practically beaming.

Still watching his wife and daughter, Rocky said, "So if I were to consider getting out in a couple of years—"

"You've got a job with GAPS whenever you're ready. Hell, I'd be more than happy to have you." Jon answered the unfinished question.

Rocky finally yanked his gaze off Izzy and turned to Jon. "Thanks. Good to know."

EPILOGUE

"The training's going well." The guilt of the lie he told his wife sat heavily in Rocky's chest.

Through the cell phone pressed closely to his ear he heard Izzy draw in a breath. "Okay. Be careful. I love you."

"Will do and I love you more. Talk soon and kiss Lola for me. Bye." He disconnected the call and glanced at Jon.

The moon lit the night just enough Rocky could see Jon's brows were lifted high. "Training, huh?"

Rocky shrugged. "What was I supposed to tell her? That my friend and I are roughing up her ex-boyfriend so he leaves town?"

Things had been going so well for them. In the past week Isabel had enrolled at the local college and they'd scheduled their first counseling session with the base chaplain—part of the deal for the man to perform their ceremony on such short notice.

Everything was moving in the right direction except for Tito. He hadn't moved on at all, as evidenced by the fact he and two of his men were still hanging around the area.

Jon held up his hands, palms forward. "Dude. I'm not judging."

Rocky rolled his eyes. "Whatever. We doing this?"

Jon snorted out a short laugh. "We're all just waiting on you."

He blew out a breath and nodded to the six-man team of GAPS operatives Jon—going above and beyond to help—had assembled.

GAPS had grown beyond the small group of Jon's former SEAL teammates. Rocky didn't even know some of the guys currently leaning on the vehicle waiting for Jon's order.

They were all geared up for what looked more like war than just roughing up a couple of Miami thugs holed up in a Virginia Beach motel.

Business being slow this time of year for the owner of this place was working in their plan's favor. There were two other cars in the lot, parked all the way down at the other end of the building. Only one other room of the eight-unit motel had lights on inside.

"All right. Let's move." Rocky reached to pull the mask down over his face, pausing long enough to say, "Remember, I get Perez."

Jon pulled his own mask down. "You can have

all three if you want. We're just here to back you up."

That was fine with Rocky, as long as he was the one to put the fear of God into that bastard who'd hurt Izzy.

Jon gave the signal and the team moved in, stacking up three deep on each side of the room's doorway as Rocky had the pleasure of breaking down the cheap door.

It seemed like overkill as the team moved in on the three shocked men. In white undershirts, with their shoes and gun belts off, they'd obviously settled in for the night.

Too bad for them.

Rocky moved in on the man he recognized as Tito Perez from his mug shots. As the team subdued the two others with little effort, Rocky delivered a single punch to Tito's face.

He heard the crunch as bones cracked and blood flew.

Tito cradled his nose in both hands, muffling his voice as he delivered a string of words Rocky knew enough Spanish to recognize as curses.

Finally, Tito said through what had to be a mouthful of blood, "What the fuck? Who are you?"

This was the part where Rocky had to employ his acting skills. He couldn't say what he really wanted to—that if Tito didn't leave Izzy alone Rocky would have no problem taking him out completely. But this area having its share of drug and gang problems gave him a good ruse to get Tito out of town.

"My boss says you've overstayed your welcome, Perez. This is his territory. You and your friends need to leave. Tonight."

Tito frowned as the blood pouring from his broken nose soaked the front of his formerly white T-shirt. "Who's your boss?"

"If you don't know that, then you're stupider than you look."

"I'm here to get my girl back." Tito's words stole Rocky's control.

Rocky channeled the rage. He had this guy right where he wanted him. Bleeding and broken, looking scared at the business end of a semi-automatic with Rocky's finger on the trigger.

Remembering he was in charge here, Rocky gathered his composure and snorted out a laugh. It wasn't hard. Tito really was laughable as he cowered on the bed making excuses.

"You keep making pussy a priority instead of business it's no wonder you're still a two-bit thug. Maybe my boss should do you a favor and take over your territory in Miami. Huh, Perez?"

Rocky heard Jon chuckle behind him.

Maybe the performance was a little over the top, but Tito needed a wake-up call. If this didn't hit so close to home and his wife's fear of this man wasn't a constant presence on his mind, Rocky might have really enjoyed this little encounter.

Tito shot a quick glance at his two men, who hadn't said a word. Not surprising. Two of Jon's team had them each in a headlock while the others covered the room with their weapons.

"Okay." Tito nodded, wiping at the blood under his nose. "We'll leave tonight."

Rocky nodded. "See that you do."

Another surge of victory-fueled adrenaline hit Rocky hard as he backed toward the doorway.

"Take their weapons," Jon ordered, taking control of the room now that Rocky was visually sweeping the motel's lot to make sure their exfil was clear.

As per their training, the entire thing took barely five minutes.

With two men left behind in a vehicle parked off on the edge of the lot to make sure Tito did indeed do as he'd promised and left town, Rocky sat in the passenger seat of the SUV as Jon drove him and the rest of the team away from the scene.

"You did good." Jon shot him a grin.

"Thanks." He'd rather be shooting bullets than shooting his mouth off but it had all worked out.

A call came through the cell phone connected to Jon's dashboard Bluetooth. He hit the button on the steering wheel to answer the call. "Rudnick."

"Perez and his men just got into their car."

"Good. Follow them to the state line and check in with me if anything changes."

"Got it, boss."

Jon hit the button to disconnect and shot Rocky another glance. "That didn't take them long. Looks like we're good."

"Yeah. Thanks for everything." Rocky turned to look at the three guys crammed in the back seat. "All of you."

Jon grinned. "You're welcome. It was good training for everyone."

Speaking of training . . . Rocky remembered his lie to Isabel. He pulled his cell out of a pocket in his tactical vest and glanced at the readout.

Jon caught the move and smiled. "Go ahead. Call her and tell her you're on your way home. I think we're done for tonight."

Rocky blew out a shaky breath, fighting the adrenaline that still gripped him. He hit redial and pressed the phone to his ear.

When Isabel answered, he said, "Hey, baby. I'm coming home."

Hot SEALs

Night with a SEAL
Saved by a SEAL
SEALed at Midnight
Kissed by a SEAL
Protected by a SEAL
Loved by a SEAL
Tempted by a SEAL
Wed to a SEAL
Romanced by a SEAL

For more titles by Cat visit CatJohnson.net

ABOUT THE AUTHOR

Cat Johnson is a top 10 *New York Times* bestseller and the author of the *USA Today* bestselling Hot SEALs series. She writes contemporary romance featuring sexy alpha heroes and is known for her unique marketing. She has sponsored pro bull riders, owns a collection of camouflage and western wear for book signings, and has used bologna to promote romance novels. A fair number of her book consultants wear combat or cowboy boots for a living.

Never miss a new release or a sale again. Join Cat's inner circle at catjohnson.net/news.

Made in the USA
Lexington, KY
27 April 2016